The Fall of Declan Curtis

John Jeremiah

ABSOLUTELY AMAZING eBOOKS

ABSOLUTELY AMAZING eBOOKS

Published by Whiz Bang LLC, 926 Truman Avenue, Key West, Florida 33040, USA.

The Fall of Declan Curtis copyright © 2017 by John Jeremiah. Electronic compilation/paperback edition copyright © 2017 by Whiz Bang LLC.

All rights reserved. No part of this book may be reproduced, scanned, or transmitted in any form or by any means, electronic or mechanical, including photocopying, recording, or any information storage and retrieval system, without permission in writing from the publisher. Please do not participate in or encourage piracy of copyrighted materials in violation of the author's rights. Purchase only authorized ebook editions.

This is a work of fiction. Names, characters, places, and incidents either are the product of the author's imagination or are used fictitiously, and any resemblance to actual persons, living or dead, businesses, companies, events, or locales is entirely coincidental. While the author has made every effort to provide accurate information at the time of publication, neither the publisher nor the author assumes any responsibility for errors, or for changes that occur after publication. Further, the publisher does not have any control over and does not assume any responsibility for author or third-party websites or their contents. How the ebook displays on a given reader is beyond the publisher's control.

*For information contact:
Publisher@AbsolutelyAmazingEbooks.com*

ISBN-13: 978-1945772399 (Absolutely Amazing Ebooks)
ISBN-10: 1945772395

To CC
Who inspired me to write this novel.

The Fall of Declan Curtis

N'attendez pas le Jugement dernier. Il a lieu tous les jours.

Do not wait for the Last Judgment. It takes place every day.

- Albert Camus

Prologue

The New World

THEY SENT an absurd stretch limo to pick Yossi up at Kennedy Airport. A bored driver in a bad suit slouched at the gate. He held a cardboard sign with Yossi's name on it.

"I'm Yossi," said the twenty-six-year-old boy.

"Come," was all he got in return.

His family had emigrated to Israel after the 1948 War. Aside from Lebanon, he had never been outside his native land. The flight from Tel Aviv was long and boring but he could not sleep. He dreamed of visiting "the largest Jewish city in the world."

"Where are you taking me?"

"To hotel."

The man seemed angry to Yossi. He gave up on conversation. He kept looking around for the famous skyline and the iconic buildings he knew from pictures, the Empire State Building, the Chrysler Building, and the World Trade Towers. But all he saw was an endless low-rise Queens landscape of sad little buildings and sooty gas stations. When they finally pulled up to a faded waterfront hotel in Brighton Beach, the weariness of the trip caught up with him.

"I pick you up at eight. You will meet your uncle at party."

Yossi felt a little better after sleeping. The concierge at the desk was very helpful. He explained that the dreamscape of Manhattan was just a few miles away and across the river. There would be plenty of time to see it all. The driver arrived on time and silently delivered him to a garish restaurant. The limo door was opened by a big man in a shiny suit. He was as gregarious as the driver had been sullen.

"Yossi, welcome to United States. I am your second cousin, Shimon," he said as he hauled the boy into the darkness of the nightclub.

A great, vulgar banquet was in progress. They said it was for him. In Little Odessa, celebrations were loud and theatrical. Conversations were delivered in fortissimo and with much physical contact. The hugging and kissing was accompanied by endless rounds of vodka and salutes.

Countless people introduced themselves as his cousins. Some were very beautiful and were not queasy at all about their putative shared gene pool. Tatiana was especially affectionate. He was not used to such freedom and sexual aggression at home. She had his attention. They danced wildly amid a crowded floor of sparkling revelers. His satin shirt clung to his soft body as if he had been doused with water. Late in the evening she enticed him to accompany her to the stretch limousine in the parking lot.

"I like you, Yossi. I like you a lot. Let's go to limo and I'll show you."

Yossi was disoriented but he didn't hesitate for a moment. The cool evening air revived him somewhat as they exited the club.

"Yes," Yossi thought. "This will be a night to remember, maybe even to brag about."

Their shoes made sharp, crunching sounds on the loose gravel and broken glass. It was dark. She stopped him just short of the limo and kissed him more passionately than he had ever known.

He didn't hear the two men until she released him. The first knife went under his lower ribs. She turned away and slowly started to walk back to the club.

Yossi made eye contact with the man who wielded the second knife. He tried to say "Why?" but a plunge into his stomach took his breath away. He was looking up at his

John Jeremiah

assailants now. They didn't stop stabbing. It occurred to him in his last seconds that the sounds reminded him of a butcher shop. Yossi relaxed and quickly bled out onto the filthy macadam of the New World.

Tatiana checked her makeup in the wall mirror. She looked at her watch to make sure it was all over outside. Then she screamed.

"Help, please help! My boyfriend is being attacked outside!"

Chapter One
The Port

THE MORNING SUN scorched through eight foot windows facing the bay. I had a pulsing throb in my brain and a thirst that could only come from three days in the Sahara or consuming a bottle of single malt. It had been some months since I was near a desert. Nineteen-eighty-eight was proving to be a difficult year in my life.

I dropped my feet over the side of the bed and tenderly held my head between my hands, hoping to keep my brains inside. Normally, I enjoyed rising early. English breakfast tea was my morning beverage. Coffee right away was somehow too coarse.

The brilliant sunrise shimmered on the bay. I lived in a six story brick mill building, one of the many remnants of the Merrimac Valley's nineteenth-century heyday of manufacturing. When I discovered this forgotten port at the mouth of the Merrimac River, it was a time capsule of the Yankee past. The people spoke a distinct dialect with echoes of Elizabethan English. The main commercial street was largely boarded up and property values were laughable. All that was rapidly changing.

The promise of a scalding hot shower coaxed me from bed. I started some water for tea and raced for the bathroom. After setting the tea to steep, I drank half a quart of orange juice. Then I dragged myself into a stall the size of a walk-in closet. It was lined with slate. Several nozzles pounded me from three directions. I stretched my arms against the walls and waited for the beating to get everything alive and circulating again.

The bright tea eased the pain of waking up. I leaned on the granite window sill and watched hungry gulls swooping below. The steely glints of sunshine on the scalloped water were hypnotizing. I let my focus blur. Patterns of light formed rhythms like music. I loved this time.

That was why I had left the windows undraped. Only when I put myself to sleep with a bottle of Macallan did I regret it. This was happening too often now, since my wife had taken off with a local sailor. He was evidently a great lover who bedded most of the desirable ladies in town. Also, Gator was a close friend.

The rattle of the freight elevator announced visitors. Passengers were expelled into a wide, ill-lit corridor. We leased one floor of the semi-abandoned mill as a group. Living spaces were walled off in a freewheeling pattern, all construction done illegally by each communal tenant. I was expecting a visit from my closest friend. Gus, to the best of my knowledge, had not bedded my wife. He was a taciturn man of few, and often blunt, words. He would have fit well in a Bergman film. He managed my affairs while I was in Switzerland.

"Hey, Bubba, had enough coffee yet?"

"I'm floating but I'll do another."

"I'm leaving on Lufthansa the day after tomorrow. Can you drive me?"

"Sure, but it'll cost ya."

"Right, put it on my tab."

My business was acquiring antique oriental rugs and selling them to European buyers. My first business ventures involved restoring seventeenth and eighteenth-century homes in the Port. This evolved into an interest in antique furniture and oriental rugs. It was providing me with a decent income. Then I met Magdi, a Coptic Christian from Egypt who spoke five languages. He had discovered two things. First, the tribal rugs that European collectors sought were nearly worthless in America. The second thing he learned was that Persian Herez carpets, disdained by

John Jeremiah

Europeans, were wildly popular in America. Thus, a business opportunity presented itself. All he needed was a partner. This mirrored the old Yankee tradition of bringing manufactured goods to the Far East and returning with tea and silk. An alliance was formed, Phoenix LLC. In five years we had done several million dollars' worth of business. During those five years I had developed an expertise in rare collectible tribal rugs, so I became a buyer as well as a supplier. Now the Soviet Union was coming apart. No one knew where that would lead. Many Russians were finding ways to get wealth out while confusion reigned. Oriental rugs were flowing into Western markets. Phoenix LLC was involved in that trade. I was due in Zurich in two days.

    I had a suite at The Storchen. This quaint hotel is on the canal just off the lake. My room overlooked the water. Its restaurant had an open kitchen with a wide rotisserie upon which succulent marinated lamb patiently turned until called for. A classic European square with cobblestone paving fronted the hotel. I looked forward to the lamb. Years of this commute taught me not to drink on the flight. I only drank sparkling water. We landed around eight a.m. I would take a hot shower and go directly to bed. In this way, I shook off jet lag and could make my first appointment over dinner with a clear head.

    Magdi showed up on time. The Copts are an ancient people, Christianized by Mark the Evangelist himself. But living in that Moslem milieu had invested him with a puritanical attitude. This evening he was happy to eat lamb and discuss tomorrow's business. But he drank no alcohol at all. Fortunately, he did not seem to begrudge me.

    "We are meeting with Aaron in the morning. He'll join us for coffee after his tennis games and then we can go to the zollfreilager, the free-port, and look at the new shipment."

    "What's the deal with tennis?" I asked.

The Fall of Declan Curtis

"His friend is a Persian guy with a retail store. They play tennis three or four times a week."

It was still relatively early when we finished. I promptly bedded down. I would be alert and ready to go in the morning.

Chapter Two
Ayatollahs

WE MET AARON AT A CAFÉ. I was ready for coffee. I also had some cheese and air-dried meat. There would be no American style bacon and eggs until I got home. Aaron had an easy and friendly way about him, even when we were in the midst of bargaining.

"After we're done here, I'd like you to meet Muktar Zadeh, my tennis partner," he said for my benefit, "and see his retail shop."

"What sort of material does he deal in? Can we do some business?" I asked.

"Sure, he deals in authentic old pieces. He likes tribal things and he buys a lot from me."

It was a stylish store front, very modern and minimalist. The contrast with the rich colors and textures of the carpets only increased their impact. Everything was clean and ready to go. The stacks were studies in perfect geometry.

"I think you know Magdi," Aaron said as Muktar nodded, "and this is his friend, Declan Curtis, from the U.S."

"You can call me Deck."

"I'm pleased to meet you. Let us have some tea," Mukhtar purred.

Of course we were offered tea, despite having just come from a café. If one chooses to live in this world, tea was one of the endless offerings which had to be accepted graciously.

Work tables were set up at the back of the room with carpets draped over them. Old men with beards worked diligently with strong but twisted fingers. I had no doubt that these men were master weavers before I was born.

The Fall of Declan Curtis

Despite their concentration on the work, I could feel their eyes on me. I tried out my disastrous pidgin Farsi on them. No dice. Not a word of reply, just a momentary glare. Hagiographic pictures of the Ayatollah Ruhollah Khomeini hung over their heads.

"They don't speak any English," Muktar said as he rested his arm across my shoulders and steered me to some French gilded chairs. We had tea and biscuits. Muktar placed a cube of sugar between his front teeth and slurped his tea through it. His skin was very brown and there were wide black rings around his eyes.

Finally, it seemed to be time to do some business. I could not suggest this. By custom, I needed to seem as disinterested in buying as he was in selling. So, I gradually worked the conversation towards my business activities. After this slow dance, he suggested that I look at a few things that might interest me. The ice was broken. Young boys appeared. Stacks were pulled down. He wanted me to make a pile I would purchase. I preferred to do it American style and get a price on each piece as we went. This annoyed him. The process took almost three hours. In the end, I had an attractive stack of tribal rugs and bags. They added up to forty-two thousand dollars. I was satisfied. We had been bent over the rugs like men in a crap game. I stood up and stretched.

"No", he said abruptly. "Not enough."

I was surprised at first, but I assumed this might be a ploy to squeeze a little more *baksheesh* out of the blue eyed devil.

"What more can I do for you, Muktar? I have chosen what I want and you agreed to the prices."

"Take these, too." He toed a stack of things I was interested in but had found his prices too high.

"You'll make the price better?" I asked hopefully.

"No, last price. You take them."

John Jeremiah

"I don't want them at that price. Let's just finish what we agreed to. It's a good start for the future."

"I don't do business for less than fifty thousand dollars."

"Really, Muktar, you won't take my money?"

"All or nothing."

I wouldn't be treated this way. I had no tolerance for abuse since my wife left. I was not naturally short-tempered. This was the new me. I had developed a careless tolerance for violence and confrontation. Magdi and Aaron were now jabbering away in Arabic and French. Things were getting out of hand. Once the elaborate customs of politeness were cast aside in that culture, violence was only a whisper away. Like a sheep dog, Magdi herded me towards the door. Aaron placated his friend. The repair men stopped working. They, and the Ayatollahs, were glaring at me with hatred.

"You've wasted my time!" I growled over my shoulder.

That set him off. He was spitting out something incomprehensible at me in Farsi as he pushed through the door. I faced him on the cobblestoned street.

"*Arschloch!*" I spat, since he knew German and I couldn't think of anything sufficiently insulting in Farsi. We went at each other furiously, but briefly. Our companions separated us and we let them.

~ ~ ~

When the three of us got to Aaron's office, we started to relax.

"I'm really sorry," Aaron said, "I've never seen Muktar like that. He's like a brother to me."

This seemed rather naïve to me. I knew men from both ethnicities and they were rarely "brothers."

"When are you leaving?" Arron asked.

"I'll be here another week. I leave on Sunday."

"Don't worry, I'll go see him in a few days and

The Fall of Declan Curtis

straighten it out. Something must have been bothering him."

"What do you make of that behavior this morning?" I asked Magdi after we left Aaron and were alone in the street.

"I am upset. You cannot fight in the street like that in this country. That is for garbage people. If it had gone on longer, the police would have had many questions. It's not good. Please, never again."

It was two days before Aaron called.

"We have to meet him at Muktar's shop; I think something is wrong," Magdi said to me.

I guess Aaron needed someone to stand with him and confirm that his nightmare was real. It seems that much of Muktar's inventory was on consignment from Aaron. Quite a bit of what I wanted to buy actually belonged to Aaron, so he had some leverage. They had reached an agreement. Muktar would sell on the terms we had agreed upon. He would meet Aaron in two days for tennis. But when Muktar didn't show up, Aaron did a short workout at the gym and showered. Then he went to the shop, looking for his "brother." It was completely empty.

Everything, every table, needle, light and rug was gone. The Ayatollahs were gone. Several hundred thousand dollars' worth of Aaron's family's rugs were gone. All flown, Aaron would later find out, to Iran.

No Israeli Jew would have any legal chance of prosecuting someone in Iran.

Chapter Three
A Proposition

AARON WAS UNDERSTANDABLY UPSET when we were last together. He dreaded the call to Haifa. But tonight, just two days later, he had recovered his composure. He told us the call had been made. Other than that, he was not going to discuss the event. It was behind him, he announced, and dinner was before us. More than once, Magdi or I attempted to gently prod Aaron on the subject of the larceny. He refused until the end of the meal. Perhaps it was the wine, but he cryptically stated that "Uncle is taking care of it." He left that for us to interpret.

"However, I do have something I would like to talk to you about, Deck. There is no secret about this information and I don't mind if you are not interested. It's just that you are in a perfect position to do a job for us and pick up a nice commission."

"Well, as long as you don't mind me telling you to go to hell, I'll listen to anything."

Despite his Western veneer, this figure of speech seemed to take him aback.

"You know my family is from Russia," he began slowly, still pondering my slang, "We have rugs and icons to sell. But we've developed a problem in New York. A distant cousin has not sold a shipment we entrusted to him. He has not made any payments. Uncle made a deal with him to return the rugs. Your position as a trader who travels back and forth from New York makes you an ideal intermediary. The cousin wants some financial compensation for "expenses." I'm not going to lie to you; he is blackmailing us for the return of the rugs. Uncle agreed to give him a hundred and fifty thousand dollars to cover his expenses.

The Fall of Declan Curtis

We need someone to take it to him, get the rugs, and export them to us."

"OK, what's in it for me?"

"We'll pay you fifty thousand dollars for a successful transaction."

I let that hang in the air for a few moments.

"No, you'll pay me twenty-five thousand dollars now, which is mine regardless of the outcome. I will do everything in my power to make things work. Then you can give me the other twenty-five if I'm successful."

"I really don't know. I think it's possible, but only Uncle can make that decision."

"Fine, you can let me know. I won't be losing sleep over it."

Aaron excused himself. Magdi and I said goodbye. My plane was in the morning.

The *flughaven* was bright with sunlight. The crowd was thin and I was early. I felt great. I had box-seat tickets for the Red Sox in three days. I wore a baseball tee shirt in anticipation of warm weather at home. The spring weather had been fine in Zurich but my foreign friends would have been shocked if I had worn short sleeves. After my wife left, I got a tattoo. It would have caused cultural confusion had they seen it. The subject of the ink was not a problem. It was the very existence of a tattoo on someone respectable that would have upset them. Magdi, for instance, would have considered such defilement the province of "garbage people."

I was two hours early. I had settled down with an Elmore Leonard paperback. I was just getting into it when I heard my name. I was being paged. When I finally got to the right phone, it was Aaron.

"Listen, Uncle wants to meet you. There is an El Al first class ticket to Tel Aviv and a hotel reservation waiting for you. Even if you two don't come to an agreement, he'll send

John Jeremiah

you home first class from there. And, he'll pay you two thousand dollars for your time if you're not interested." He hesitated a moment then added, "But, even if you're not interested, don't tell him to 'go to hell.'"

    I smiled. Some things just don't translate well. First class would be nice. Two grand for nothing would be nice. I gathered my things. I glanced at the mirrored wall and saw my tattoo, a quote from the legendary Delta Blues man, Robert Johnson.

Chapter Four
Uncle

THE FLIGHT to Tel Aviv was four hours. No matter what happened, the delay would not be more than a day. I'd be at least two grand to the good and on a first class fight to Boston. What could possibly go wrong? The sunlight was blinding as I slipped on my Ray Bans. I grabbed a cab to the Rothschild Hotel. The eponymous avenue where the hotel was located was laid out in 1910. The oldest architecture in this bustling commercial hub was located here. Fleeing German-Jewish architects brought the Bauhaus aesthetic to the city in the 1930s and filled this neighborhood with smooth modernism. The Rothschild was a modest three story hotel in an indistinct Deco style. It was well-kept. I only did the briefest luggage drop before descending to the bar on the first floor. Being on "retainer" shouldn't prevent me from enjoying some Macallan. I was in the habit of ordering the twelve year old. It was eminently drinkable, easy to find in most bars, and not overpriced like the eighteen year old that I drank at home. Of course, I had it neat in a rocks glass. The bartender did a slight double take.

"Yes, just malt, just a rocks glass, no ice." In many locales, if one didn't ruin the single malt with ice, it arrived in a dainty stem glass. That's fine for cognac but not for whiskey. That didn't jibe with the bartender's expectations from my accent. I'm sure he anticipated a demand for a sub-arctic malt, drowning in water. Nonetheless, he delivered a decent pour with no chitchat. I liked him already.

I was just easing into a second one when a serious young man stepped up to me without hesitation. He looked like a "crowd man" for the secret service. Not a stand-out cop, but squared away enough to draw the attention of someone who was trying to avoid it.

"Mr. Curtis?"

"I'm sure you already know the answer to that, chief."

"Uncle is ready to see you. Please go to Penthouse 4, at your leisure."

"At your leisure" seemed to be a term of art. He made no move to depart or even back off. He simply hovered and looked blandly at my drink. If I were in an armchair he might have sat in my lap. I was determined not to be hustled along. But in the end it was more felicitous to simply down my Scotch and follow him. To my surprise, he only escorted me to the elevator. I rose alone. A jacketless young man awaited. A Beretta was clearly visible at the small of his back as he ushered me to Uncle. The term "penthouse" seemed a little grand but there was a comfortable outdoor deck.

Uncle did not rise, but he smiled warmly and extended a hand like a movie star. I took his hand and produced my best business smile. His eyes were behind opaque sunglasses. My gaze fixed upon his shaven skull. It was somewhat knobby like an old wrestler. He had that kind of a body as well, not even remotely soft but filled out as strong men became in their fifties. He was bear-like.

"Mr. Curtis, a pleasure to meet you."

"Thank you, sir. I don't know why it is a pleasure for you, but I'm grateful. Please call me Deck."

"Well, my boy, we'll see how we do together and then we will decide what you may call me."

I didn't quite know how to respond to that non-sequitur.

"I bring greetings from your nephew, Aaron."

"Ah yes, poor boy. It's not nice that he was taken advantage of. Not nice, and I may add, neither wise nor safe."

I got his message clearly.

"Sir, you've gone to some effort and expense to have

me here. I've heard your nephew's version of your motives. But it just doesn't add up."

"You're a smart man Deck, and I have taken the trouble to find out about you. Of course, fifty thousand dollars is a lot of money to do something any drug mule or accountant could accomplish for a few grand."

He stopped and leaned back into his armchair. He seemed to be letting the words sink in. Maybe he was calculating his next revelation. He offered me a Cohiba. It was a six-inch Corona, a size I preferred. We both did the licking and cutting and lighting dance. Smoke began to rise in the warm sunlight.

"Shlomo, bring me some water." He had neither turned his head nor raised his voice.

The security man appeared with a tray. Uncle had quinine with ice and lime. There was a crystal rocks glass with three neat fingers of Macallan in it, even though no one had asked. Then he disappeared.

"I'm not going to lie to you Deck. There's been some trouble. If you'll let me tell you about it, I think you'll see that you are in a situation to help me and profit yourself."

"I'm here to listen."

"My family made a fortune running clothing factories in Russia. Our main customer was the military. We lost money making uniforms for them on the day shift. But in return for a consideration, they kindly ignored us as we ran the factories at night. We paid the workers double what they got during the day. The goods we made were sold on the black market. Everyone was happy and we became rich."

"Sounds like a creative way to co-exist with Communism."

"Yes, it was fine for a long time. But now the Soviet Union has destabilized. I'm sure you understand what's going on. The family decided it was time to get out. I won't bore you with the details, but we began to convert our capital into icons and rugs."

"I'm not bored at all," I said, "may I ask why you chose those commodities?"

"It would be too difficult to move cash out of that system. Like Hemingway's fish, it would be consumed in little bites along the way."

I was surprised that this man would have that allusion at his fingertips.

"So why the rugs and icons?"

"We wouldn't have the expense of converting currency for our purchases. They can be bought cheaply there. No one knows their worth in the West. And there are many Southern routes out of the USSR that are less controlled. The officials don't know what the values are so they can be bribed cheaply to let us export."

"And once you have them out?"

"We have a perfectly legitimate import export business here. We ship to various free-ports in Europe and the goods are sold. My nephew Aaron is only one of our outlets. As we convert the goods back into capital, our family can re-invest in real estate in the West."

"That's damned interesting, really. But where do I come into you plans?"

"A cousin of mine, Oleg, is a gangster. He is dangerous, stupid, and he is not alone. In Brighton Beach there is a powerful Russian mob, and he is an underboss. I did not realize that he would challenge me like this. I gave him very favorable terms. He could have made a fine profit if he had done his job. But he has become corrupt and lazy. He decided to steal from me and dare me to go against the organization he has joined."

"That sounds very dangerous. But if you know about me, you know I'm just a small entrepreneur. I'm not any muscle at all. I don't see where I fit in."

"I like you, Deck. And I said I'm not going to lie to you.

John Jeremiah

So, here's the worst part. Originally, Oleg agreed to return the goods to me for some 'expense' money. I sent my nephew Yossi. They murdered him."

For the first time, Uncle showed emotion. Two veins pulsated on his left temple and an angry color flushed his pate. In a supreme act of will, he drew a deep breath and smiled. Oddly, this smile seemed infinitely more genuine than his first greeting.

"Sir, why would you think I'd do this? If he would murder his own blood, what value would my life have?"

"Of course, Deck, of course. You are perfectly right. But know this, we are not animals like his mob in Brooklyn. But we are not weak either. You should know that Muktar is already recovering in Tehran from a crippling injury to his leg. No more tennis for him. His associates are returning our goods, along with some 'expense' money for us."

We took our time. We drank our drinks and smoked our cigars while those words filled the empty space. I pondered rough justice. Then he leaned forward in his chair and rested his elbows on his knees.

"Look, I am just a business man. I never indulge in rackets or violence for profit. But in our land, in our historical situation, there is no authority to turn to. We must protect ourselves and our family fortunes. It is not unlike your American West in the nineteenth century. The more a man had, the better prepared he needed to be to defend it. So, I want you to know that Oleg realizes we will go to war unless he settles with us. He will not hurt you. I have explained to him that no matter what the cost, we would arrive in force and wipe them all out. Now, they simply want to finish with us."

"So, if they kill me, keep your rugs, and steal your hundred and fifty grand, I will have the satisfaction of knowing you will try to kill all of them."

"I think we are beginning to understand one another,

The Fall of Declan Curtis

Deck. There is another thing. I know about your father and his connection to the New York Police and the FBI. I will make sure that Oleg realizes that, too. He will know that harm to you will bring tremendous pressure on them from those directions as well."

"I see, I'm your ideal neutral agent. And I have additional backing of my own. Well, logic is on our side," I said, "but people don't get into mobs because they are smart. They are frequently slow-witted and short on impulse control. I could end up dead for one of many stupid reasons, not the least of which is your cash. But for the first time I think I have the whole story."

"Anything could happen to us at any time Deck. I think your odds are OK on this one."

"You know my terms?"

"Yes, they're fine," he relaxed and drew on his cigar, "I understand you have a tattoo?"

I rolled up my sleeve for him.

I been mistreated
An' I don't mind dyin'

"It's from Robert Johnson, an American genius."

"Yes, I had someone look it up and explain it to me. I understand the sentiment. We'll get along fine."

He smiled for the third time and chuckled.

"Pardon me. I was just thinking that the Nazis would have liked your arm as a lamp shade. Shlomo will give you your airline tickets and cash."

"A hundred and seventy-five thousand?"

"No boychik, you'll get your twenty-five thousand now. He'll give you instructions about where to pick up the rest in New York. Good luck. And you may call me Uncle.

Chapter Five
Help

WHY WAS I GETTING INVOLVED in this dangerous enterprise? I knew it had something to do with my wife. Alcohol took the edge off my anger and humiliation. But this new adrenaline rush was even more satisfying. Instead of being dulled with booze, I felt alive and stimulated. I was smart enough not to be romantic about the morbid world of thugs. This wasn't a movie. I knew underworld types. I understood exactly how obtuse, violent, and mundane they were. But sitting with "Uncle" on that sunny veranda made me feel like I was in a movie, talking to Myer Lansky in 1959 Havana. Well, maybe I wasn't so smart after all.

Twenty-five grand was not chopped liver, but I didn't need it. The second twenty-five would make it somewhat interesting. But I would only get that if the deal was completed. If the deal busted, chances were I wouldn't be entertaining a dinner party with that adventure story unless the celebration were convened in hell. I hadn't intended to take the job. Then he made it clear that he knew all about me. He knew about my family's connection to law enforcement. With a middleman the mob couldn't kill, the deal could be consummated without starting an expensive war. Suddenly I realized why I was worth fifty large to him. And I also knew they probably wouldn't kill me. Probably.

I had a pistol and a concealed carry permit in Massachusetts. It wasn't hard to get. I was well-known in town and they were issued by the chief of police. I simply told him I handled large amounts of cash in my business. And I presented a safety course certificate. I wanted to have protection with me until this adventure was over. I would have to find out what I needed to do to take it to New York.

The Fall of Declan Curtis

    I liked my Walther. An uncle of mine who was vacationing in Germany in 1943 took it off a German soldier "who didn't need it anymore." It was a small .32 caliber Walther PP, ideal for discreet carrying.
    I dragged my suitcase up to the loft. Broken clouds darkened the water in the bay. Random shafts of sunlight descended through the gaps. Summer was approaching. White sails dotted the waterscape. A sixty foot schooner made its way through the narrow channel into our harbor. It was under sail and engine power. It would take another twenty minutes to cross the bay and find a mooring up river.
    I opened a beer and flopped into a leather armchair. It would take about two weeks for my purchases to arrive and be guided through customs by my broker. A trucking company would deliver them to our warehouse. So, I had a two week window in which to do my assignment.
    "Hey Bubba, you in there?" I heard Gus shouting.
    "Bubba" was an interchangeable term for anyone we liked.
    "It's open," I said.
    "Got one of those for me?"
    "You know where they live."
    Gus sat with his, drinking from the bottle.
    "Everything went fine while you were away. Paperwork is on your desk, nothing unusual."
    "How about you? Is your charter schedule filling up?"
    "Yeah, July is full and August looks good. I even had a few days out while you were away."
    His boat was a thirty-eight foot wooden trawler built in 1957. He had restored it so meticulously that is was hard to believe it was an old boat. I remember when I first boarded her when he was done. He took me into the bilge and it was a spotless red cradle of wood. But that was Gus, an obsessive perfectionist who would not hesitate to re-do any work that did not satisfy him. All the bright work was

mahogany. The cabin had clever storage cabinets, a small top loading refrigerator, a compact stove, and an impossibly narrow shower. The salon had generous mahogany trimmed bunks and an elegant built-in desk with cabinetry and drawers. A Mossberg over and under shotgun was mounted in a glass-fronted mahogany case over the bunks. The aft deck was a roomy platform for lazing in the sun, fishing, or eating a feast. Gleaming in patterned gold leaf on the mahogany stern was her name, "Shinola".

"My business went fine. But I got myself into some extra-curricular activity that could prove dicey. I'd like to tell you about it."

He sat through my recitation. By the time I was done he had drained his beer and started another.

"That's the worst idea you've ever had. I know you're not happy right now, but this shit will pass. Getting yourself killed won't make anything better."

"I'm not planning on getting killed."

"So why are you doing it? You don't need the money."

"I guess I can't explain it. I wasn't going to do it but I'm hooked in now. I guess it's just the first time I've really felt alive since the shit went down. Adrenaline is more powerful than alcohol. Are you going to help?"

"Personally, I could understand if you wanted to kill Gator. But killing yourself seems like a twisted sort of revenge."

"Well?"

"Of course I'll help. I'm not going to just sit around and wait for news of your demise."

"Thanks Bubba. I've got some ideas about how to get away with this."

"Another fine mess you've gotten us into," he said in his best imitation of Oliver Hardy.

Chapter Six
Red

MY DAD was a tough, funny, and smart guy who grew up in Brooklyn. He handled the political affairs of John Jay College of Criminal Justice. He was a man whose opinion you naturally wanted to live up to. Five high-ranking NYPD detectives had their gold shields mounted on a plaque for him when he retired early because of a heart attack. When he died, hundreds of people filled the church where he was married and I was baptized.

One of the gold shields that now hung in my office was Red's. I had made arrangements to meet him at The Landmark on 11th Avenue. This was a nineteenth century wood frame building not far from the college. It had never been anything other than what it was now, an Irish neighborhood tavern. I ordered a pint of Guinness and some potato and leek soup. It had a perfect texture and I didn't mind the bits of bacon they floated in it. I ate too much Irish soda bread while I waited.

"Declan, how are ya, boyo!"

He was a shortish, compact man and walked with a slight roll, like a sailor. I rose to shake his hand.

"Red, it's grand to see you. It's been since we buried the old fellow."

"Nobody's over that, Deck. It'll never be the same there without him."

"Well, 'you can never step in the same river twice.' Life goes on, even without the most 'indispensable' of us."

We exchanged pleasantries as he settled into his beer. I knew he would do anything for me or my family for the sake of his late best friend.

"Well Red, you're not going to like this story, but here it is."

I told him I had been hired to do the exchange. I did not

The Fall of Declan Curtis

tell him about Yossi. But I made it clear that these were shady characters I was dealing with.

"No, no, this is all wrong. Forget about it. Give them back their money. Nothing is worth getting killed over."

"Nobody's getting killed Red. They want my boss's money and he just wants his goods."

"Nothing is ever that simple when you're dealing with scumbags. Look, if it was that simple, they'd just have scumbag lawyers do it."

I laughed. He was right, of course.

"And what's going to happen to your pretty little wife if you get killed?"

"Well, that ain't my problem anymore. She ran off with a sailor."

I tried to make it sound flippant but he saw right through me. He was a detective, after all.

"Oh, I'm sorry to hear that, Deck."

He was so Irish, there would be no further questions or "feeling my pain." That's what I like about us.

"Look Red, what I want to know is, if I can carry here. I've got a concealed carry permit at home…"

He was already shaking his head.

"…and I was wondering if I could get something here."

"Not gonna happen. Maybe if you were a big movie star or the Governor's nephew. But the Sullivan Act is the toughest law in the country. It's ironic since "Big Tim" Sullivan was a thug himself, but there it is. You carry here, and it's a felony. No way around it. I can't help you."

"Can't you get me deputized as temporary private eye or something?"

"You've been watching too many movies, boyo. Forget it."

"OK. Well, if I decide I need some muscle, I'll hire a licensed P.I. Can you give me a few names?"

"Sure." Red said. As he scribbled three names on a

business card he grinned.

"You know, they say Big Tim passed that law because the hoods in the Five Points gangs complained that their victims were starting to shoot back."

"William Burroughs said that after every shooting spree they take the guns away from the ones who didn't do it."

"Who's William Burroughs?" Red asked as he handed me the card.

"A guy who did it; he shot his wife."

"Listen, don't do this. I'm not your old man, but we both know what he would have said.

Just don't. And if you do, keep me informed of when and where. There are plenty of people who would still do anything for your father, even save your foolish ass."

"OK, thanks Red," I said. I felt bad about lying to him.

Chapter Seven
The Bear

OLEG WORRIED when the Boss called. He knew Yissakhar didn't like him. Even worse, he knew the Boss considered him to be a slow-witted liability. While Bogo brought the Town Car around, Oleg checked himself in the mirror. He centered his tie and bared his teeth. He brushed some lint from his jacket. He peered at his lumpy face. He didn't look for long; he knew he was a little grotesque. He simply wanted to be sure there wasn't anything obvious to annoy the Boss.

"I understand you have a new arrangement with your Uncle."

"Yes, Boss, I do." Oleg looked around the office. He was nervous. He hadn't been invited to sit.

"It was stupid what you did with the last one. It was stupid that you didn't let me know your plans. I am speaking from my heart when I tell you that I don't know why you are alive before me now."

Yissakhar, The Bear, the big boss, leaned back in his chair. He let those words work their magic. Clearly, Oleg didn't know what to say. The Bear thought Oleg was beginning to tremble. That pleased him. He stood up abruptly and Oleg involuntarily shrank. That satisfied the Bear. He walked to a sideboard and poured himself a Johnny Walker Black on the rocks. He didn't offer anything. He glared over his drink.

"Nothing must go wrong this time. I don't want a war over your petty shit. You give that bastard his goods and end this. What is he giving you?"

"A hundred and fifty."

"OK, do it. No trouble. Just finish it. And then you bring

The Fall of Declan Curtis

me half. If anything goes wrong, you're all dead."

"It's all set, nothing will go wrong." Oleg said with a faint note of pleading.

Yissakhar walked over. He stood too close to his underling. Oleg smelled the Bear's scotch and aftershave as he desperately tried to avoid eye contact.

"Is it possible that you don't completely understand me? Can you possibly think there will be a next time or even a tomorrow if anything goes wrong?"

"No, no, I understand you completely. Trust me. Everything will go fine. Just a simple exchange."

"And my money."

"Yes, of course boss, that's understood."

"Leave." he said.

Bogo was waiting in the outer office. He stood as still and almost as large as a mountain. They walked down the empty hall to the car.

"We need two yeggs to drive the goods to Red Hook and pick up the fee. I don't want geniuses," Oleg said to Bogo.

"How about Sammy and Bud?"

Oleg looked uncertain.

"They dumped two trucks in Jersey for us. And a little fire in Bensonhurst, too."

"Right, OK, I remember. Don't tell them too much. They'll figure there's money in the package, but don't say how much. And make our meeting soon afterwards. Don't leave any time for ideas to happen to them."

Oleg was silent for the rest of the drive. Goddamn it, why had he made things so complicated? He could have just sold the goods in the first place. Or, he could have taken the fee and returned the goods to Yossi. Instead, he murdered and robbed his second cousin. Why? Did he want to challenge his Uncle? Did he want to show how powerful he had become in America? If so, he was the

John Jeremiah

fool. The only power he had was Yissakhar's, and now the boss was ready to kill him. He didn't want to think about it anymore. He just wanted it to be over.

Chapter Eight
The Ambush

THE MONEY was in the rug district. Gus and I had rooms nearby at the Carlton. The office was a disheveled storefront with piles of worthless rugs and a flat top desk. The old man behind the desk didn't sell rugs. He bought checks. It was an internal credit system in the trade. Wholesale merchants sold to retailers on credit terms. The retailers gave checks dated in the future. They usually ranged from one to three months. The old man bought the post-dated checks from the wholesalers at a discount of a few percent per month. I actually knew this factor. He had occasionally held some of my paper. We nodded at each other.

"Shalom, Mr. Gohari."

"Shalom, shalom, Mr. Deck. How are you?"

"I'm fine. Do you know why..."

He held up his hand to stop me.

"Here," he said and reached into his desk and put a brown leather shaving kit bag on the desk, "take it in the back."

In the tiny back office there was a huge safe, a plain table with no drawers, and an electric money counter. Mr. Gohari's young assistant nodded politely and took the bag. The one-fifty was in hundred dollar bills. They were wrapped in paper bands. He broke the first wrapper and fed the bills into his counter. Each packet was ten thousand. Each one was only a centimeter thick. When the fifteen packets were counted and re-wrapped, he put them on the table in a stack.

I was amazed at how small it was, six inches tall, just three pounds. He didn't touch the money again. He gestured that I should take it. I put it in the kit bag and had

The Fall of Declan Curtis

room to spare.

"Do I need to sign anything?"

The assistant shook his head and pointed to the high tech cameras that covered the room from two angles. I was a movie star.

~ ~ ~

Gus had the BMW running when I came out. The hand-off was at eight p.m. in Red Hook. I still didn't know exactly who I was dealing with. But they would have a rental truck with the goods and one car to leave in. We were to have one car and one driver with me. The rendezvous was in the center of a vacant lot, so they could see that no one else was coming. Simple.

"I feel guilty, leaving the boys stuck in the back of that panel truck while we luxuriate."

"They'll live, but you're going to owe them," Gus said.

The box truck had been at the edge of the lot for a few weeks. It was stripped but the box was intact. We were glad to find it. Our four man crew had been in there all day with coolers and slop buckets. They didn't want to be spotted coming and going if the lot was being surveilled. The back doors were locked from the inside. They had drilled holes in the side to watch us from. I hoped they were ready for action and not bored to sleep.

"All right, let's get started," I said.

"Listen man, you're going to be out there alone. If anything happens, just give it up. Fuck it, don't be a dead hero."

"Stop being an old lady. By ten o'clock tonight we'll all be eating catfish at Sylvia's, on me."

"I'm havin' ribs," Gus said.

"Now you're talking. Just keep that happy thought."

~ ~ ~

They were there and waiting in a Ryder truck. A Honda sedan was nearby for the drivers to leave in. Gus slowed to

John Jeremiah

a crawl while we scanned the lot. Our secret weapon was in the distance. That made six of us and two of them. But now that I envisioned myself alone at the truck, our team seemed far away. Gus let me out. The thieves were standing at the driver's door. As per our agreement, Gus drove back to the entrance.

"You got the money?" A potbellied slob asked in a lazy monotone.

"Sure I do, you think I'm out here for a picnic?" I waved the leather kit at them.

"How about a quick peek at the goods?" I asked.

They looked at each other. They seemed uncertain. I didn't move my hands. The Walther at the small of my back was a comfort.

"Sure you can. Unlock the back, Bud."

We moved to the back. Bud reached up to the lock. I watched him fiddle with it. It was foolish of me to let myself get between them. His friend hit me hard from behind. I lurched forward into Bud and slid to the ground. The big guy kicked me twice in the side. The kit fell loose. I couldn't see where I was as I rolled away from the kicks. I found myself under the truck and drew my gun. It may have been premature, but I fired anyway. I could hear squealing tires. I hoped it was friendlies. I fired again, but I couldn't really see where they were. I kept scrambling around, looking for feet. Then I saw our boys from the box truck running towards me. They fired a couple of shots. The thugs fired at the BMW and hit the radiator and blew the windshield. The truck started up. I rolled away from the wheels and found myself on top of the money. The thugs traded more shots with our guys but were gone in minutes.

I was relieved to see Gus out of the car and on his feet. He had glass shards on him but no blood.

"Come on, get in, we can catch them," he shouted at our crew.

The Fall of Declan Curtis

"Stop, stop. Now who's trying to be a dead hero? You gonna chase them with an overheated radiator and a busted windshield? You'd be lucky if the cops didn't shoot you. Let's just get out of here, now!"

We split into three groups and exited the lot on different sides. We left the BMW right where it was. I'd report it stolen in the morning. We met where our crew left their car. They dropped us back to the hotel. At least I had the money.

Chapter Nine
The Mess

BOGO GOT THE CALL from Sammy. It sounded all wrong.

"Bogo, the bastard brought a crew to the exchange. They damned near killed us, but don't worry we still got the goods."

"You don't have the money?"

"No, you don't understand. They tried to rip us off. They tried to kill us."

"Did you clip anyone?"

"No, they took off......"

Sammy was eager to go on, but Bogo wasn't interested.

"Shut up and listen to me. Bring the goods right back to the warehouse where you got them. We'll be waiting. Be there in one hour, exactly."

Sammy started to congratulate himself on saving the load but there was no one there to listen.

"What?" Oleg roared when Bogo told him.

Bogo had never seen him like this. Oleg was trying to speak but his words came out like animal sounds. He was spitting and turning purple.

"S..s..sons of bitches! Have some muscle meet us there in twenty minutes." Oleg ordered.

The warehouse was only a few blocks from the Navy Yard. It was four stories of poured concrete. The Town Car's tires rumbled on cobblestones as they approached. The overhead door began to open for them. Bogo pulled into the darkness and away from the door. He swung the car around and pointed the high beams at the entrance. Two silent goons were already there, standing at attention. Oleg didn't know their names and didn't want to. Bogo went over and whispered to them. They unholstered large automatics and stepped into the blackness behind the Lincoln.

"Get ready to open the door. And keep them covered from behind," Oleg said to Bogo who pressed his back to the concrete wall.

Twenty minutes later they heard the old box truck bouncing on the uneven pavement.

Bogo started the roll-up door. Bud and Sammy pulled the truck towards the glaring headlights of the Town Car. Both men were trying to shield their eyes. By the time they stopped the truck and got out, they were squinting like moles. The overhead door shut behind them.

"This way," Oleg said.

They stumbled toward the voice.

"Everything is here boss, they didn't touch..."

"Shut up! Now, one of you tell me, slowly and clearly, what happened."

"The bag man brought a crew. They tried to jack us. We're lucky we didn't get killed."

Oleg looked at them a long time. He paced in front of them like a penned up animal.

The drivers were uncomfortable. The boss looked like he smelled dog shit.

"You don't look lucky to me," Oleg said in a sort of low growl.

Bogo stepped up from behind and whacked Bud unconscious. He turned his gun on Sammy.

"If you're holding, you better give it to me now."

The driver hesitated just a moment. Bogo knew Sammy was calculating his chances against Bogo and Oleg. That moment ended when he saw the two goons emerge from behind the Town Car.

"Sure, sure, we're all on the same crew here."

John Jeremiah

Sammy slowly drew a .38 from his overcoat.
"Don't hold out on me," Bogo said.
"No, no problem. That's all I got."
"OK, what about him?"
Sammy rolled Bud over and pulled a cheap Saturday night special out of his pocket. Bud began to stir. Bogo took the piece and herded them to the back of the garage. The goons tied Bud to a concrete column. They gagged his mouth with a rag and tape.
"All right. First of all, your story is bullshit," Oleg said, "The bag man was an FBI brat. The only thing he ever jacked was a piece of college ass. But that's OK, we're gonna find out exactly what happened. Poor Bud, he can't tell us, even if he wanted to. He's got a little speech impediment now. So, it's up to you."
"I swear, they jumped us and, and.."
Oleg took pruning shears out of his pocket and tossed them to one of the goons.
"Finger."
Sammy looked on in horror as Bud lost his pinky. The goon tossed it at Sammy's feet.
Bud tried to scream under his gag but only choked. His wild, desperate eyes pleaded with his friend. Although Bogo had a gun on Sammy, he sensed the driver was about to run. Bogo grabbed his collar and kicked his feet from under him.
"Kneel."
Sammy was kneeling before Bud when his friend's ring finger went. This one bounced off Sammy's chest.
"Listen pal, what's your name?" Oleg asked.
"Sammy."
"OK, Sammy, he's gonna run out of fingers. Then it will be your turn." Oleg waited a few beats.
"Or maybe we should ask your pal if he thinks you should take the punishment for a while?"

The Fall of Declan Curtis

This clearly appealed to Bud. He started to shake his head like a bobble doll. Sammy deflated.

"OK, Boss, OK. We tried to grab the money. But we saved your goods. We would have split the cash with you, I swear."

"Kill them. Leave them somewhere they will be noticed. We'll make it clear that stealing from me is a death sentence. Do it tonight. Leave nothing here but the truck." The goons just nodded.

"Please..." Sammy started just before Bogo knocked him out.

When they got back to the office it was after midnight. Oleg had Bogo come in. He poured them drinks.

"Here's the situation. If Yissakhar finds out about this, we're all dead. He promised to kill me and my entire crew if anything went wrong. There's no good or easy way this is going to come out. I've got to tell the boss I got the money and gave over the rugs. Then I've got to give him his half!"

Oleg started to pace.

"Seventy-five-thousand, of my own goddamned money," he screamed at Bogo.

Oleg seemed to regain control of himself after a while. He spoke to Bogo in a calm and reasonable tone.

"How did things get so fucked up?" He mused as if it were a philosophical question.

Bogo knew his boss didn't expect an answer. He waited.

"All right, the goons need to disappear. I need you to do it. I'll give you some cash to 'pay' them. You can do it then. Just leave 'em where you drop 'em. It doesn't matter who finds them. You can keep the cash."

"Sure boss."

"Then, I gotta ship that crap back to Israel like I'd been paid." His calm tone started to slip. "Son of a bitch, I hate this whole fuckin' thing!"

John Jeremiah

He poured two more drinks. Bogo declined.
"Gotta be ready when the boys call for their pay," Bogo said.
Oleg went to his safe.
"Here's ten grand. Make 'em go away."
Oleg seemed lost in thought for a few minutes.
"And then there's the kid. After you finish here, I need you to go to Boston. Find him, get my one-fifty, and kill him. No need to hide him. Just do it clean and get out. Then, only you and I will know what happened. I know I don't have to tell you, but nobody can know about any of this. Yissakhar has to think everything went as planned."
Oleg watched Bogo's back as he left the office. He'd be hard to replace. But it was just business. When Bogo was dead, only Oleg would know the secret. He chuckled to himself. It would be like it never happened. Yissakhar and Uncle had no idea how smart he was. He went back to his desk and finished the drink Bogo had declined.
"Vechnaya pamyat."

Chapter Ten
"Silence Stares"

IT WAS FIVE DAYS since they tried to kill me. My side still ached from the kicks. I was spending a lot of time on the sofa with Emily Dickinson. She's a deeper gal than she gets credit for. "When everything that ticked has stopped, and silence stares all around..." Those words chilled me. Silence was staring at me now. I had no idea what to do next. I still had the money. The gangsters still had the rugs. We had set up surveillance cameras to cover the hall and my fire escape. I knew they'd come. It was just a matter of when. My .32 rested on Emily's collected works. I had no way to reach Uncle. I just had to wait.

"Hey, did you read the *Globe* today?" Gus asked when I picked up the phone.

"No, I've been involved with an older woman who's taking up most of my time."

"I'm pretty sure those meatheads who jumped you in Brooklyn just turned up dead."

"Why is that in the *Globe*? Thugs get dumped all the time."

"They left these guys in the park. They wanted them in the news."

"I have no idea what's happening. Could Uncle have gotten to them already?"

"Remember what Bill's Greek mechanic always said?"

"Yeah: *'who's fuckin' know?'*"

I got my ass up off the sofa and walked to the kitchen like an old man. I un-wrapped some triple smoked bacon from Karl's Kitchen. The Germans called it "ready to eat" bacon, but I gagged at the thought. However, with the application of some heat, the rich smoky flavor improved all

The Fall of Declan Curtis

food. I diced chunks and sautéed them. I whisked up three eggs and poured them into a cast iron skillet, sizzling with olive oil. I added the bits and some grated Parmigiano-Reggiano, and folded that little bit heaven into my breakfast. Never mind that it was after noon. I was in the middle of a food orgy when the phone rang again.

"Tell me something good."

"Is this Declan Curtis?"

"Indeed it is. Sorry if I sounded too casual."

"I have a message from your Uncle."

"OK, you've got my undivided attention."

"Your Uncle has received his property. I would like to deliver his appreciation."

I really didn't know what to say. Was this a hit?

"Listen, this got very complicated. Can I explain it to Uncle myself?"

"It's been very nice speaking with you, Mr. Curtis, but I have other obligations. I must see you today."

His precise and formal diction made him sound like an English butler.

"Where?"

"I am in your quaint village. I can come to your loft, or you can tell me where else to meet you."

"OK, I'll see you at the Grog bar in an hour."

"That will be satisfactory."

I called Gus and asked him to populate the bar with a few friendlies. I cleaned and re-loaded my Walther for the second time that day. I took my time getting there. No one likes to be first to a party. Although I had made the mistake of not asking how to identify him, there was no problem. He sat at the bar, dressed like an undertaker, sipping a Pellegrino. I didn't let that passive exterior fool me. Professional assassins rarely look like monsters or mug shots. He spoke first.

"Mr. Curtis?"

John Jeremiah

I sat down, keeping one stool between us.

"You have the advantage of me sir."

He didn't seem to feel the need to identify himself.

"Your Uncle is satisfied. I will excuse myself in a moment. When I do, I will leave this briefcase behind."

"Wait a moment. What does this all mean?"

"I have told you everything I know. Good day sir."

I reached out and grasped his forearm. He looked at me as if I had grabbed his ass.

"Don't," he said, and he wasn't asking.

I let go.

"Look, I've had some people try to kill me. I'm a little cautious."

"That is always distressing. What do you want of me?"

"Can you open that thing?"

"Here is the key."

"Will you open it for me?'

"I'll do anything to get out of here."

We walked over to a private booth. He lifted the case on to the table and inserted the key. It made a nice little mechanical snap and he lifted the lid. I immediately closed it and picked up my twenty-five thousand dollars.

"Good day, sir."

~ ~ ~

I tossed the briefcase on the floor of my loft. I had given part of the first twenty-five thousand to the fellas who kindly prolonged my stay in this vale of tears. I had the hundred and fifty parked in Gus's safe deposit box. It seemed that Uncle had his goods. I felt there was a bigger game being played here than I could grasp. Why did Oleg send the rugs back without the ransom? And if he intended to send them back anyway, why did he try to kill me instead of just taking the money? I decided to seek the advice of an eighteen-year-old. As usual, the Macallan allowed me to relax and think clearly. Although I pondered the situation

The Fall of Declan Curtis

through several re-fills, I failed to achieve enlightenment. However, I did achieve a blissful nap.

There are many odd noises in an old mill building. The rudest is the rattling of the freight elevator and the groaning of its cables. There are the shouts from various arguments or love making, and other celebrations by tenants. There was the out-of-tune piano, occasionally accompanied by a real singer. And of course, there was the scrambling of our little four-legged roommates. It's curious how you adapt to all that racket and sleep undisturbed. But a noise that you haven't heard before can rip you from the warm arms of Morpheus. Such was the scraping sound from the metal door to my fire escape. Adrenaline brought me right off the sofa. Something wasn't right. I reached for the Walther. Yes, it was definitely at the metal fire door. Unfortunately, the dead bolt was in the open position. There was only a simple cylinder lock between me and my guest. I made it over to the video monitor. I couldn't see his face. He was bent over the lock. Then it clicked. He stood up. He was big and he was uninvited, and he was holding a .45. There was no time to analyze. Just as the door began to move outward, I kicked it with all the leverage I could manage.

My guest exhaled like a fighter after a solid body shot. I knelt down and assumed a two-handed firing position. The half-opened door rocked slightly on its hinges. The outside lamp lit an empty iron platform. I stared stupidly at the night. I moved to the wall. Approaching from the hinge side of the door frame, I could see down the steps. They were empty. I reached out and swung the door until it hit the iron railing. No one there. I looked all around for my phantom. The only sign of his visit was a .45 on the floor grating. I leaned over the railing and peered into the alley. There he was, quite corporeal although somewhat worse for the four story trip he had taken. I carefully picked up his automatic without touching it. I put it in a big Ziploc bag.

Then I called Gus.

Chapter Eleven
The Body

GUS AND I muscled the body into his panel van. A dead body is a damned awkward load, especially when the live version weighed three hundred pounds. I had to find out who sent him. Assassins in movies carry no IDs. Our man had a wallet, two credit cards, a few hundred bucks, and a driver's license from New York. I guess he didn't consider this a very high level hit. The name on the driver's license was Bogolyubov. We went upstairs to call Red. We both needed a drink. Gus was a Bourbon drinker and always *kvetched* about my "effete" single malt. But he never turned one down, or even a few.

"Listen son," said Red after I gave him a *précis* of the evening's events, "you're in a lot of trouble. Your old man never would have let you get started on this bullshit."

"I know Red, can you find out who this guy is?"

"I know damned well who he is. He's Oleg's man, they call him Bogo."

"What does he do?"

"He does whatever Oleg tells him to do. He was probably one of the knives on the Yossi hit. Yes, I know about that, too. You have a problem. When Oleg finds out Bogo is dead, he'll just send another hit man, maybe a team. You're screwed son. You have to get out of the country. You need a new name. Oleg's a lot older than you. These gangsters don't usually get to be old men. You'll just have to wait him out."

"Fuck that, no two-bit Russian thug is going to ruin my life."

"Sure, blow off some steam now, but use the little bit of time you have to think this over. You need a plan. If you

The Fall of Declan Curtis

ditch Bogo's body, you probably have about a week before Oleg sends out scouts."

"You don't care what we do with him?"

"He's a hired killer. We know of at least a dozen of his hits. You killed him in self-defense. Maybe you didn't even kill him; maybe he just slipped and fell on his own. The point is, we don't care if you sell him to a dog food company. But take that week and make a plan. Oleg's not going to go away."

"Thanks, I understand," I said.

"And let me know what your plan is. If they get you, I promise I'll get them."

Why does everyone think their revenge will make me feel better about being dead?

~ ~ ~

I straddled the doorway to the Shinola's wheelhouse. I was trying to massage some of the aching muscles I had strained while moving that meat-mountain around. We had backed the van up to the floating docks where the Shinola was moored. The marina kept a few carts for bringing coolers and groceries on board. They were deep plywood boxes with large bicycle wheels. A high pipe-handle was attached to one end. Bogo was in a tarp which slid pretty easily off the truck bed and into the cart. But getting him out of the cart was almost as hard as getting him into the van. The boat bounced angrily and pulled at the spring line as he hit the deck. It had been our plan to put him in the storage bin that doubled as seating on the Shinola's deck. But the idea of getting him in there, and out again a few hours later, became distasteful to us. We decided to keep him rolled in the tarp and pile some ropes and anchor chain on top. He'd just look like poorly stowed equipment in case we had to talk to the Coast Guard.

The Shinola was moving through the jetties and into the Atlantic just before the sun broke the horizon. She had a top speed of eight knots. It would be hours before we reached Jeffrey's Ledge, a long plateau under the Gulf of Maine. It's a rich fishing ground. Gus thought Bogo should sleep with the cod. I felt bad dragging Gus into this. I tried to soothe my conscience by thinking he could only be charged with tampering with a body.

"Here."

"Thanks," I said as I took the mug.

"We'll use an anchor chain to weigh him down," Gus said.

"Won't that just unwind?"

"I've got a couple of shackles. We'll make a nice, tight bundle. He'll be like a roast for Sunday dinner, only this meal is for the fish."

"Thanks for that image. It may be a while before I eat fish again."

"If you knew what fish ate, it would make sausage seem like tofu," Gus said.

"I'm really sorry I got you involved in this."

"Shut up. Don't go all dopey on me. If that scumbag had killed you, who the hell would I drink with? Anyway, if some mad dog came after me, you'd be right there. So, enough bullshit. We're not having a spiritual crisis here. We're just taking out a load of garbage. If you can't deal with that, then you should've let him kill you."

"Bubba, I'm surprised people aren't flocking from all over to benefit from your wisdom and guidance."

"How do you know they aren't?"

He said that with a sidelong glance and I knew that subject was retired. For the next few hours we said very little. We enjoyed the motion and the air and the light. We went through a quart of orange juice after we tired of the coffee. We ate some hard boiled eggs sliced on toast with mayo and ground pepper. We ate a melon, too. We never played music at sea, only if we were anchored somewhere

The Fall of Declan Curtis

and settled in for the night or for a meal. Just being out there, far out there, was a fully engaging experience. In the best of weather, the colors of the water or the leaping fish or hunting birds provided ample amusement. In poor weather, our concentration was fully centered on the danger we were in. It wasn't panic, but it was a type of controlled fear. Gus always knew what needed to be done. I was very good at following orders.

There was a special feeling when you can only see ocean in all directions. The tiny boat becomes your world. Leave that world and the bigger world will eat you. I suppose you could say the same for our planet, this tiny spec floating in a universe vastly greater in proportion to our planet than the ocean was to our boat. But that was too vast to grasp. A thirty-eight-foot bit of wood in a quirky ocean full of creatures looking for a meal was a metaphor on a scale anyone could comprehend.

Bogo dropped quietly into the soup when we finally managed to get him over the rail.

"Better you than me," was all I could manage.

Chapter Twelve
Dolus Eventualis

BEN FRANKLIN famously said that three people could keep a secret, as long as two of them were dead. I had to keep this to myself. I told Gus I was going for an interview with Red. Maybe I was lying to myself as well. I was going to Brooklyn to confront Oleg. I wasn't about to spend my prime years hiding from him in a foreign country. So, I needed to get to him before he realized that Bogo was gone. I was on my way alone to corner a minor mob boss who was trying to kill me. What the hell did I think was going to happen? I didn't want to think about it. I had Bogo's .45 with me in a plastic bag. On some level of my consciousness I knew why. It was the same reason I had the latex gloves. But I was detached from that scenario. I felt like Camus' stranger, maybe it was the sun.

I checked into a Sheepshead Bay motel and paid cash for a week. "The United States of America" on the bills was the only address they required. I had my leather Ghurka bag with me. It was packed with several days' worth of black tee shirts and underwear. I spent the first night cleaning my Walther. I also carefully unzipped the plastic bag and slid Bogo's .45 out onto a towel. I pulled on the latex gloves. I carefully picked the cannon up without smudging the grip. And expelled the clip. It was full. Everything looked clean and oiled. I made sure it would work if I needed it. In the morning I had my hair buzzed very short. The change was stunning. I had also gone without shaving since the attack and the shadow of my beard changed the shape of my face as well. If anyone did remember seeing me around the club, they would never recognize me with a shave and normal hair. I returned to the room and showered. I never liked the feel of clippings under my shirt.

I spent two days getting a feel for Oleg's routine. I saw how he entered and exited his office in the night club. I knew his Town Car and its license plate. Oleg never took this driver into the building; he always stayed with the Lincoln. On the evening of the second day, I waited behind the club. I had my .32, Bogo's cannon, and a crow bar. I had made arrangements through a "friend of a friend" to have someone sideswipe the Town Car. They only knew the make, the place, the plate, and the time. The car came by two minutes late and scraped the Lincoln. I'd hoped that distraction would give me time to slip into the stairway to Oleg's office. But I hit the jackpot. Oleg's driver pulled the Lincoln into traffic and gave chase. I had to laugh. I took a leisurely stroll to the doorway. I looked around quickly and jammed the bar into the frame. The tongue of the lock popped right out and I was in.

It was only ten, so there was still plenty of club noise throbbing through the building. I didn't worry about stair noise. It was more important to get there quickly. The upper hall had four doors. Only one had light spilling out under it. I pulled on the gloves. I took the .45 out of the bag. I took the safety off and checked the chamber for the third time. I got ready to kick the door. Then I wondered if a knock would work. Finally, I tried the door knob. It swung open noiselessly. I assumed a crouched firing position.

Oleg sat behind his desk facing me. He was wide-eyed. I stood and kicked the door closed behind me.

"Just put your hands flat on the desk where I can see them."

Oleg was clearly surprised, but not upset.

"Sonny, do you know who I am? This is the worst mistake you've ever made. Anyway, we don't keep any money here, look around. If you leave quickly, I'll let you live."

John Jeremiah

"I know exactly who you are. You tried to kill me."

Now he was interested. He squinted at me as if he were trying to see through something.

"You're the kid. Son of a bitch! What are you doing here?"

"I want to know what's going on. Why did you try to kill me and then send the rugs back anyway?"

"It's a long story. Believe me, it wasn't me who tried to hit you. It was all a mistake. The yeggs who did it are dead. That should prove to you that it wasn't my idea. You're OK and Uncle has his goods. There's nothing to be worked up about," he said in a soothing voice, " why don't we relax and have a drink? It's all over now. There's no reason why we can't be friends."

He started to withdraw his hands from the desk.

"Don't," I said.

"Relax sonny. Of course, I have a gun in the drawer. Let me roll back out of reach. There's nothing to fight about. It's over. Let me roll my chair away from the desk. I'll stand up and you can frisk me. Then we'll have a drink together and be friends."

I let him get up. He smiled at me like a shark and moved to the sideboard.

"Killing someone is the easiest thing in the world," Oleg said over his shoulder as he pulled out glasses, "Look at you, I don't know how you did it, but here you are. You got to me. And you don't know anything about this life. I have power at my disposal that you can't imagine. If I wanted you dead, you'd be gone already. What'll it be?"

"Scotch, neat."

He started to pour. I wondered how he would take the news.

"This is Bogo's piece," I said as I waved the .45.

He threw the decanter. He pulled a revolver from the sideboard and started to raise it. I shot him twice before

The Fall of Declan Curtis

he hit the floor. I didn't have to check. Two .45s in center mass were plenty, despite what you may have seen in movies. I was starting to hyperventilate a little. I set Bogo's gun down. I removed the gloves, took out my .32, and left the room. The shots didn't seem to have attracted any interest. I walked out the door in the most nonchalant manner I could muster. The Lincoln had still not returned. I put my head down and walked back to my hotel.

Chapter Thirteen
Mending

MY FRIENDS SAY I am mending since my wife left. "Mending", of course, is a relative term. When someone gouges out your eyes, you do not grow new ones. But you can learn to find your way in the dark. Indeed, I've been operating in the dark for some time now. I had willfully put myself in this situation. Did I want to die? Not exactly. Robert Johnson was closer to my feeling, I just didn't mind dying. I had been betrayed by a woman I had chosen to spend my life with. My faith in my own judgment was challenged. I'd spent fifteen years with a stranger. And I deeply trusted the man she left with. We had sailed together and drunk together, and tempted fate together. I was profoundly disillusioned. Now I had killed two men.

Yes, the first one was trying to kill me. His misadventure was not intentional. But there it was, I killed him. I handled his body. It was truly personal and disturbing. I would never have crossed paths with him had I not engaged upon this fool's errand. Killing his boss was not as innocent. Oleg was certainly a monster. But I had preserved Bogo's gun and fingerprints. I knew in my heart that at least one of us would not survive our meeting. Do they have a category for pre-meditated self-defense? I'm certainly guilty of that.

Yet the evidence, Bogo's .45 with his fingerprints, will convince everyone that Oleg was on the short end of a falling out with Bogo. The mob will look for Bogo for a long time. Killing an underboss cannot be tolerated. But the police will only spend a few weeks looking for Bogo. Then they'll assume he's either left the country or been found by the mob.

The Fall of Declan Curtis

And even if everything goes my way in the end, I'll still be left with this burden. I will never be the same man I was. Blood never washes off. I had volunteered to be a part of some dirty business. The life and death excitement blocked out my pain and humiliation better than any booze or other drug. But I had lost my innocence. There was no moral high ground. It was easy, and true, to say that they were monstrous sociopaths. But what was I? I was a mercenary who had lain himself down with dogs.

And yet, the people I had signed on with were relatively innocent victims. Uncle had lost an innocent nephew. He was the leader of a stiff-necked people, but he was the victim of crimes rather than the perpetrator. In the case of Muktar, Uncle's version of self-defense was ruthless. But if he had not been wronged, he would not have wreaked his stern vengeance.

And then there was the hundred and fifty thousand dollars. Uncle had willingly paid that for the return of his goods. He had received his goods. My mission was accomplished. Everyone living was satisfied. Everyone who knew otherwise was dead. If not a murderer, I had at least become a killer. Should I become a thief as well? Certainly, I had been paid well for my services. If I had theoretically delivered the goods without paying for them, did I not earn the ransom money?

Parsing the act of theft in this case felt like parsing my killings. Maybe keeping the money could be justified since everyone got what they bargained for. On the other hand, could I play this game at Uncle's level? If I fought out of my weight class, I could wind up like Muktar, without a leg to stand upon. And even if I didn't mind dying, did I want it to be over a pointless theft?

From my loft I can watch the business of pleasure sailing in the harbor. I also enjoy watching storms develop. Often in summer, black clouds roll down the Merrimac

John Jeremiah

Valley through our port and out to the ocean. Sometimes, the sun sheds warm yellow light on us while the black storm approaches like doom. You can see walls of water sheeting down on the landscape from ten miles away. Finally, the air begins to turn. The roar of rain is accompanied by booming thunder as the cold air from the mountains collides with our warm coastal atmosphere. Then all hell breaks loose. This isn't drops of rain by any definition. It is an absolute deluge. Water seems to pour, rushing over some waterfall in the sky. The town square fills up with several feet of water in just a few minutes as the drainage systems are overwhelmed. I love the chaos.

Chapter Fourteen
"Six Hundred Pounds of Sin"

I WAS DRINKING a pint of Guinness at the Grog and anticipating a hamburger. A couple of bored looking detectives called Paul the bartender over. They flashed their IDs.

"Have you seen this man around here?"

Paul bent forward, pulled his long hair back behind his ear, and looked closely.

"No, definitely not. But I'm not here all the time."

"Of course. Is your manager in?"

"Not until four."

"OK, let me give you a copy of this picture. Give it to your manager. Can you do that for me?"

"Sure, no problem."

"Have him show it around, maybe pin it up in the locker room."

"Her."

"What?"

"The manager is a she. I'm sure she'll be glad to help out."

"Here's my card. Call me if you get any hits, will you?"

"You bet. My name is Paul. Can I get you something?"

The lead detective hesitated, looking at my hamburger as it arrived. These were famous burgers. But his partner, who looked like he had already eaten several dozen doughnuts, suggested that they canvass the other bars in town before they sat. He got over-ruled and they perched a few stools away from me.

"Is that as good as it smells?"

"You won't be disappointed." I told the detective. I decided not to engage in any further conversation until I

The Fall of Declan Curtis

heard why they were here. I knew Paul would chat them up.

The Grog burgers were well seared on the outside and topped with bacon and cheddar and served on an English muffin. Half way through his feeding frenzy, the detective became loquacious.

"This is really great, Paul. You've got an interesting town here."

"It's a hell of place, full of artists and musicians and various dropouts looking for an easy life or a new start. What brings you here?"

"We're NYPD. We're just checking on a missing person. He left his car here."

"Oh yeah? The guy in the picture?"

"Yup, no big deal, his family just wants to know if he's OK."

After they left I nodded to Paul.

"Another?"

"You bet. Can I see that picture?"

Son of a bitch, if it wasn't Bogo in all his brutish glory. I'm pretty sure this was a blown up mug shot with the numbers cropped out. He looked like one of those wrestler characters on the Friday night fights, like Gorgeous George but without the gorgeous. I wondered if the detective meant to be ironic when he said "his family" wanted to find him.

It was the car, of course. I hadn't thought of that. Whether it was his personal car or a rental, they would have his name. I wondered now how close to my building he had parked it. Unless they stumble into someone who saw him, this should go away fast. And it's unlikely that a hit man would let himself be seen in a restaurant or hotel in the same town as the job. No, we're probably OK with the cops. I went to the pay phone.

"Gus, I'm glad you're in. I'm at the Grog and two detectives from New York are showing around pictures of Bogo."

"How the fuck did they get here?'

"He left a car somewhere in town. They didn't say where. I'm sure no one will have seen him. He would have been a ghost while he was on a job. This is just routine. They'll be gone in a day. What I'm worried about is the mob."

"Yeah, they'll have even more motivation to find him. This is bad. When they hear where he left the car they'll be all over you like a bad suit."

"Maybe you should come to the loft and we'll figure something out."

"What, you need someone to hold your hand, Mary?"

"Yeah, you got a problem with that?"

"I'll be over in an hour or so."

"Thanks, Bubba."

When I got out of the car at the mill, I couldn't resist looking around carefully. It was mid-afternoon and the streets were empty and silent. The creaky old freight elevator groaned its way up to my floor. The hall was shrouded in its perpetual gloom. Only a few industrial shades with sixty watt bulbs made navigation possible. I glanced up at my hall camera as I turned my key. All seemed quiet. I was bolting the door from the inside when it suddenly twisted my hand back and slammed into my forehead. I went sprawling back on my ass. I wasn't exactly knocked out, but my mind spun like wheels in mud without producing any ideas. Two preposterously large goons let themselves in. One of them closed the door on the shattered frame. The other one put me to sleep.

I don't know how long I was out, but when I woke up I was sitting in a wooden chair. I was roped to it quite thoroughly from my shoulders to my ankles. They had tossed the place relentlessly. On the table before me was my twenty-five grand, a few odd thousands of petty cash, some accounting ledgers and my Walther. The larger of the two

The Fall of Declan Curtis

ogres had a shaved head. He leaned toward me with a different picture of Bogo.

"Where is?"

"I don't know. He was here two weeks ago."

He slapped me with a hand that felt like a telephone book. Everything went fuzzy and my ears rang.

"Listen, you oaf. I had a job. I was a courier, you understand? I simply made a delivery."

And then he hit me again. He had grotesque prison tattoos on his hands. I started to think this could be fatal if he didn't speak English.

"It was my job to give him a package," I said as I leaned over and spat out some blood, "that's all; it was money for his boss. He came here, I gave it to him, and he left. That's all I know."

Baldy started to speak to his pal in a mumbling, gravelly sort of Russian. His friend nodded to him and drew a Glock semi-automatic. These were not common in the US at the time. The Austrian army used them to replace their Walthers. They were plastic and good for smuggling. Baldy opened a large briefcase. He took out a small propane torch and replaced it with my cash and my gun. I didn't like the direction this was going in. I started to explain again that I had nothing to tell him, but he stuffed a cotton table runner halfway down my throat and tied it tightly. He tore open my shirt down to the navel. He calmly turned the wheel and lit the gas. He looked at me with dead fish eyes as he moved the flame to my chest. I wrenched around as the acrid smell of burning chest hair cut through my agony.

For the second time that day, the door was kicked open. Gus was there with a cheap .38 he had inherited from his cab-driving uncle. He didn't hesitate to shoot the friend wielding the Glock. The damned .38 sounded like a cap pistol. I heartily approved of his choice. It was not a fatal wound, but the Glock hit the floor and he had their rapt attention.

"You, put that fucking thing out and untie him."

The friend was holding his arm now and glaring at Gus with hatred. He also seemed to be recovering his strength. His big mistake was trying to recover his Glock. Gus shot him in the thigh as he bent to get it. He went down with a whimper this time. Gus immediately trained his toy pistol at Baldy.

"You, pick up the gun and give it to me. Do it!"

Baldy shuffled over to the fallen Glock and reached for it.

"Careful now, I've got four more shots. I'll fuck you up good. Pick it up by the barrel."

He gave it to Gus with downcast eyes. He seemed very pragmatic, unlike his friend who was clearly angry now.

"Get down on your knees. Put your hands behind your head. Now!"

Gus moved towards my bed and pulled off a sheet. He tossed it at Baldy.

"Tie your friend's leg up. Let him hold a wad of sheet on his shoulder. Stop making a mess in my pal's loft."

While they busied themselves with that, Gus picked up a kitchen knife and gave it to me without taking his aim off them. I finished the job of releasing myself. It hurt to stand. It hurt to move. And the bloody blister on my chest had made me rather cranky. Gus handed me the Glock. I checked the action and the load. It was ready to go. Fortunately, I was able to restrain myself from using it. Tweedle Dum and Tweedle Dee were huddled on the floor, a six hundred pound pile of angry, bemused Russian gangster. I gave it back to Gus, who now looked like a well-armed maniac.

"You hold both guns on them. I'm going to get us a drink. If they move at all, empty the fucking things into them. I'll be right back." Then I stopped and added, " As a

The Fall of Declan Curtis

matter of fact, if you get too tired of holding those heavy weapons, just shoot them and have a seat."

I moved off to find some Macallan and my Polaroid camera.

"OK, Gus, here's some well-deserved whiskey. Please put the .38 down and hold the Glock on them."

Then I toasted him, with apologies to Mr. Hammett.

" *Success to crime,* Bubba."

"Ok, assholes. Do you want to leave here alive?"

They stared at me dumbly. I picked up Gus' .38 and stood over them. I put the gun in the friend's mouth and cocked it.

"Last chance, dipshit! If you can't understand English, I can't make a deal with you. So I'll just have to blow your fuckin' brains out now."

Baldy spoke up.

"Wait, wait, we understand."

"What about your pal?"

Friend shook his head that he understood. I withdrew the gun.

"Sorry, Gus, we got a little slobber on your Saturday Night Special."

"Hey, let's shoot 'em for that," Gus suggested.

I slowly wiped his spittle off the barrel onto the friend's left shoulder, the one that wasn't bleeding.

"No Gus, we're going to be pals now. I just need to get it through their barbarian skulls."

I filled two water glasses with four fingers of whiskey. Our guests took them with some hesitation.

"Smile, assholes," I said as I took several good Polaroids of their faces.

"Now, for Christ's sake, pay attention to me. We're going to have a quiz when I'm done. If you fail it, I'm going to shoot you. Well, in your case, buddy, we're gonna shoot you a third time. But don't worry, that'll be the last time."

John Jeremiah

He didn't care for me at all.

"Now, here's the deal. My friend Gus and I are going to make sworn affidavits that you two monsters tortured and attempted to kill me. These will be left with my lawyer, along with your pictures. I think I'll take your driver's licenses as well. The lawyer will have sworn testimony to give the police, along with your identities and your pictures if anything happens to either of us. Are you following me so far?"

They nodded solemnly.

"You see, I want to let you live. I want us to be friends."

I poured them another round of Macallan. They didn't hesitate this time.

"I'm only going to say this one more time. Bogo came here for his boss's money. I gave it to him. He left with it. That's all I know. End of story. I'm gonna let you go now. Tell it to your boss. Bogo left town with his boss' money. There's nothing else here for anybody. Do you understand me?"

"Yes."

"And one more thing. Suppose you decide to kill us and take your chances with my lawyer? Here's the problem with that. Your boss in New York will find out that the cops are looking for you. You would be the only connection between him and our murders. What will he do?"

They were reverting to dumbness again.

"You, dumbbell, do I have to shoot you again? What will your boss do if he finds out you're linking him to a murder investigation?"

"Get rid of us."

"Bingo! Give the man fifty dollars. You are so much smarter than you look. You are dead if anything happens to us. Either the cops will get you or the shmucks you work for will kill you. Here, one more whiskey for you and let's get you into a car."

The Macallan was going down nice and easy now although it seemed a shame to waste it on them.

"And one final thing, don't go to a hospital within a hundred miles of here."

After they drove off, Gus looked at me.

"You think they bought that bullshit?"

"Yeah, they're just dumb enough, and it's not like they can go to someone for advice."

"Well, wise guy, they may be dumbbells but they were just a minutes from barbequing your smart ass."

"True Watson, but it was just by chance. Even Sherlock could have a piano fall on his head. Some things are just acts of god and have to be dealt with as they arise."

"It's just a good thing I 'arose' when I did."

"Indeed, and it's a good thing you were holding the hundred and fifty K. If they had found that here, nothing could have stopped them from killing me and running off with it."

Chapter Fifteen
Gator

I HAD MOST of my affairs in order. The last shipment of rugs had been photographed and tagged as to the work required. The bales were then flown to Robert Mann's Restoration facilities in Denver for the work. I had to go back to Europe in three days for a major auction. I had some high-powered pieces consigned there in Wiesbaden. I would also be a buyer for decorative carpets which would sell better in the US market. It was a complete vacation for me, since all shipping and receiving would be done by the auction house and customs brokers. All I had to do was wave a paddle, eat extravagant meals, and go to the opera at the Hessisches Staatstheater. This Baroque Old World opera house has superb acoustics and startling intimacy. On this visit I would see a modern dress version of La Traviata. I suppose I should also mention that my hotel was a nineteenth-century resort hotel, with natural baths in the depths below, and massage tables manned by broad-shouldered older women who beat the creaks out of your bones.

I was enjoying a Brandenburg concerto and a wee dram while I pondered the hundred and fifty thousand dollars in Gus's safe deposit. More and more, I was coming to feel that we had earned it. After this last OK Corral incident, I guessed Gus had a legitimate claim to some of it as well. My reverie was interrupted by some rapping at my door. I instinctively reached for my Walther which was never far away these days. I checked the hall camera and thought my head would explode.

Gator was right before me when I opened the door. I felt my face flushing but I tried to project a calm demeanor. I thought to myself that it took some real sand to show up here.

"Well, come on in."

He let out with his ridiculous giggle that sounded exactly like Popeye and shuffled past me. I still had a drink in my hand.

"You got one of those for me?"

"Sure sport, have a seat."

I handed him a whiskey and sat back down in my armchair.

"Look, we've been friends for fifteen years," he began with forced earnestness. He reached for his cigarettes, which he chain smoked every waking hour. When we sailed together, I would hear him wake at night and light up in the dark and go back to sleep when he was done hacking.

"Not in here, sport." I told him. I confess that it was partly just to keep him as uncomfortable as possible.

"Look, we made a bad mistake. I just want to tell you, man to man, that I'm sorry. Be honest, you know you weren't taking care of her. Well, it just happened. I know I can't undo it. But I want you to know that it really didn't mean anything, really. She loves you. She really wants to come back. Please give her a break when she gets the nerve to come here."

"Is there any other bullshit *cliché* you'd like to run up the pole?"

"Come on, man. We got history. We've sailed, we've had each other's backs in bars. There ain't anything I wouldn't do for you."

"I always thought so, Gator. But what I found out is that there isn't anything you wouldn't do to me, either. Listen, man, I knew you were a snake about women. I watched you fuck with people's wives ever since I knew you. I laughed and went along with the 'he's just a good ole boy' bullshit. And then you did it to me. Well, fuck you very much."

"Look, I'm sorry. I never should've done it..."

"Just stop right there asshole. I know I own part of this. But you're the snake in the old song that the woman finds frozen and dying. She takes it home, warms and feeds it, and saves its life. Then it bites her. She asks him how he could do that. He tells her as she's dying, 'You knew my nature when you found me'."

"It's not like that, Deck..."

"It's exactly like that, Gator. What you don't know is that I'm not the same man you knew when you left here."

I stood up from the armchair. I wasn't sure what I was going to do next. I was feeling wild and restless. I dropped my glass and picked up the Walther. I didn't point it at him, but he was paying careful attention.

"It took a lot of balls to come and see me. I respect that. Now get the fuck out of here."

He rose slowly and seemed to be reaching for something else to say.

"Don't say anything. I don't know what I'm going to do about you. But I'll tell you this, we will never be friends again. If you stay here in the Port, stay away from me. If you want complete safety, I suggest you kill me when you can. Otherwise, just consider me to be a wild animal that could bite you at any moment."

Once again, he started to mouth a reply but thought better of it. Then he turned and went out of my life.

After four fingers of Scotch and some breathing exercises, I started to calm down. I called Gus.

"Hey, Deck, before you say anything I gotta tell you something. I'm just gonna say it outright. They're back in town. Joey saw them on State Street."

"I know, Bubba. Gator just left here about a half an hour ago."

"Son of a bitch, he's got balls."

"Yeah, you gotta give him that."

The Fall of Declan Curtis

"What did you do?"

"Well, he walked out of here upright and he wasn't leaking any sap."

"What did he say?"

"Sorry."

"What?"

"He said he was sorry."

"And you didn't shoot him?"

I knew Gus meant that to be funny. We weren't the kind of guys who shot people. We were just pot-smoking English majors doing our Bohemian thing. At least that's how we saw ourselves. And a few months ago that would have been accurate. But we were both different now. We were guys who had shot people and disposed of a body. And we didn't quite know how to view ourselves now; we'd never be the hippies we were again. But I didn't think we'd ever be the sort of men we had shot.

"Listen why don't you come over? I want to talk to you. I don't think you need your pop gun either."

When he got to the loft he again wanted to hear exactly what Gator had to say. I didn't blame him. It was the sort of fraught conversation that novels are made of. But I had no interest in rehashing it.

"Look, he said he was sorry. I said fuck you. That was it, end of story."

"OK, OK, no problem. But only saying 'fuck you' shows remarkable self-restraint on your part," Gus said. But I ignored him.

"The reason I asked you over is that I've reached a decision about the dough. We've risked our lives and done awful things for Uncle. We got him his goods. I've had three attempts on my life and who knows what else will come along. We did the job and earned the money. This last attack put me over. I'm keeping it. Now, I wouldn't be alive if you hadn't backed me up. So you take half of the one-fifty."

John Jeremiah

"Bubba, I'm just not going to say no. But I will say thanks."

"Don't be too thankful, we may both end up dead over this. But we'll have enough dough for a grand send-off."

There was a tentative knocking at the door. I moved to the camera.

"Fuck. You better go."

He looked at me quizzically until the door swung open.

"Anne," he said and then let the absent sentence echo in space. After all, what could you say? He passed her silently as he left.

She looked at me but clearly couldn't make noise come out of her mouth.

"Come on in. Sit down. You want a glass of wine?"

She gave me a shy little nod.

"OK, what is it you want to say to me?"

"I'm sorry. I'm so sorry."

"I'm sorry, too. Your boyfriend led off with that, didn't he tell you? Anyway, it didn't go over very well. So now we're all sorry. Anything else?"

"First of all, he's not my boyfriend. Deck, I love you, I've always loved you. Something went crazy. It didn't mean anything."

"Stop right there. You were doing fine until the 'didn't mean anything' bullshit. You two are a broken record."

"Well, of course it meant something. It meant you and I were unhappy and we didn't know how to talk to each other about it. We were sleepwalking for years. Unsaid things are often more corrosive than the harshest of words. But I love you, I would give anything if it had never happened. Please, give me a chance. I love you."

"OK, we agree on something here," I stood up and walked over to her, "I, too, would give anything if it had never happened. And I love you, it's always been you. You know that. But I can never get past this. You should have

The Fall of Declan Curtis

talked to me. It's too late now."

"Don't say that Deck, I hate myself. I'll make it up to you," she slid off the chair and wrapped her arms around my thighs. "I'm sorry, on my knees I swear, I am so sorry."

It killed me to see the woman I loved like that. I pulled her up by her shoulders.

"Don't, I can't stand to see you like that. Look, neither of us was really happy before you left. And now there's this. It's really too late now."

I reached out to the sideboard and lifted a beautiful American Arts and Crafts bowl made by Greuby. We had picked it out together and we both loved it. The matte green rim was decorated with spreading trees whose roots were intertwined. I shoved it into her hands. She looked dumbly at it.

"Drop it."

"What?"

"Drop it," I shouted as I slapped it out of her hands. It shattered on the floor.

"Tell it you're sorry."

"No, Deck," she whimpered as tears began to flow. I bent over towards the mess.

"I'm sorry," I shouted at the floor. "She's sorry, really."

Then I looked at her.

"Well, look at it. Look at it! Is it OK now?"

"No," she whispered.

"Please Anne, I'll always love you. But I don't ever want to see your face or hear your voice again. Get out of here, please."

As she shuffled down the miserable hall, I wanted to call after her, beg her to come back.

Chapter Sixteen
The New Deal

IT WAS A RELIEF to be leaving town. I hoped that whoever sent the Russian thugs to look for Bogo was satisfied there was nothing more to be learned in the Port. The New York tabloids had pretty much convicted Bogo of murdering Oleg. The gun with his fingerprints was very convincing. Now they could all concentrate on hunting Bogo down. I was sure I was out of the loop in the minds of Oleg's associates. Leaving all that behind induced a euphoria I was happy to indulge. My business class seat on Lufthansa was a mile wide and obscenely catered with decent food and endless drinks. I broke my usual flying rule and enjoyed some Bordeaux with my steak. I even indulged myself with some '63 Dow's Vintage Port which they served in tiny bottles, *gratis*.

I was headed to Wiesbaden for an auction. The train from Frankfurt passed slowly through neat, middle-class neighborhoods. Bedroom windows were opened to the spring sunshine. Eiderdown quilts and other bedding were draped over the window sills, freshening in the glorious breeze. It was a picture of domestic tranquility.

Dieter was the director of the business. I liked him. He had visited me in the Port. Our cultural differences provided us with material for friendly argument and discussion. He was an earnest man with a successful corner on the collectible market for rare oriental rugs. The tip of their spear was a fine color catalogue for each auction. He was a practitioner of orderly and honest business.

He was also unapologetic about his ancestors' SS histories. I recall him once referring to "that awful man, Churchill." When I queried him about his reasoning, he

The Fall of Declan Curtis

replied that the war could have been over much sooner if Churchill had not insisted on "unconditional" surrender terms. As much as I wanted to tell him about General Grant, I chose not to take up this fruitless argument. We were here to do business.

When I got to the gallery, I could not help but notice a congregation of loud and slovenly men on the street. They were clearly drunk and menacing and not German. I started to climb the stairs to the second floor where the galleries were located. Dieter appeared on the landing. Two workers were struggling to move a heavy desk. He began to greet me when a bottle smashed on the sidewalk.

"I told them to leave here."

Upon this declaration, he pushed past his workers and back into the gallery. He was brandishing a .38 revolver when he returned. I hesitated to get in his way as he bounded past me on the stairs. He pointed the pistol at the men and shouted at them in German. They scattered.

"It's the Poles. They are flooding the country. The ones who can't find work stay on the streets drinking. It's a disgrace."

Admittedly, the established order in Europe was under a lot of stress as the Soviet Empire gradually lost control of its satellites. The Germans did a pretty good job of dealing with security. I remember the first time I disembarked at the Frankfurt Airport and saw a heavy presence of men with automatic weapons and combat regalia. There were numerous posters with rows of mug shots featuring wanted terrorists. Many of the faces had dramatic X's over them. These folks were not kidding. Several members of the Baader-Meinhof Gang, for example, were X'd out.

In addition to my own business interests, I was covering the auction for an American magazine. The star of the event was an ancient Mughal garden carpet made with pashmina wool. It came from a famous American family but had floundered about in the New York market for a few years. Now it was recognized as the masterpiece that it was, and the rug world was waiting to see what value that the cognoscenti would assign to it. In the end it brought close to a million dollars and made an exciting story for the magazine.

When I was leaving the airport, the method of security was to line up everyone's luggage on the tarmac. We were led out to identify our pieces which were then loaded. Only then were we allowed to board. It seems naïve, now that we deal with terrorists who would gladly board with their bombs. As my plane landed in Zurich, I noticed half-track tanks on the tarmac. It seemed ominous. The military theme continued inside the airport, with serious-looking soldiers in camouflage sporting impressive automatic weapons. Their high, polished black boots reminded me of a different generation of soldiers.

"What is the security situation about?" I asked an airline employee.

"Arafat is coming to a peace negotiation."

Magdi was waiting for me when I passed through customs. His wiry hair stood up like an Afro. This punctuality was unusual. He operated on what he called "Phoenix" time. This meant being late for all events and barely on time for travel. My memories of travel with Magdi involve running madly through *bahnhof*s and airports.

"So, the Chairman is coming to town. That's a lot of upset and expense for the city."

"Yes," Magdi said, "but nothing compared to what New York pays for the UN."

"Indeed. I'm not a big fan of Zionism but Arafat is not exactly a dependable partner for a peace settlement."

"You should be glad to have him," Magdi said as he locked his gaze on me. "If they get rid of him, the ones who follow will be worse than you can imagine."

The Fall of Declan Curtis

These words, of course, proved to be prophetic.

His English was excellent. But he was always listening to my syntax and frequently remarked on an unusual word or a nice turn of phrase. Today we had a little business to attend to and then a lunch before we previewed an auction. I looked at some carpets in Magdi's warehouse and we finished up quickly. We had been doing business so long that he knew what I would buy and what I would pay. There was no need for bargaining or subterfuge. After a pleasant lunch we headed to the auction house. This was a pedestrian venue which dealt in lesser goods than my friends in Germany. However, it was a fine spot to pick up the occasional gem, since it was not so well covered by the European dealers. We had a good relationship with the owner whom Magdi had cultivated. In his office, I discovered that he had a video and intercom system throughout the exhibition space. He could overhear clients' private discussions about the lots. I was becoming somewhat inured to European corruption, although I still felt uncomfortably naïve.

"Good evening, Mr. Curtis," purred a smartly dressed man I didn't know. I offered my hand.

"How do you do," I said.

"Pardon me, we have not met."

This is the spot where most people would insert their name. He did not.

"May I have a quiet word with you?"

We took a few steps away from the nearest viewers.

"I bring an invitation from your Uncle."

I immediately thought of the intercom and suggested we exit the building.

"Uncle is in Zurich and would be pleased if you would join him for dinner."

The USSR was losing control of the edges of its empire. The Baltic states were clamoring for independence and riots

John Jeremiah

were happening in the Caucasus and Armenia. No one knew what the new Russian situation would bring. I ran over all of our dealings in my mind. I guess I still had complicated feelings about Uncle's hundred and fifty thousand. It was like having an affair with a woman who might know I was dating her sister. Was she angry? More importantly, was she armed? I told him I would be happy to see Uncle.

The Kronenhalle is a classic Swiss restaurant. The wood-paneled walls provide a warm background for its remarkable artwork. We sat at a table beneath a Chagall. The table was impeccably set. I ordered a Macallan and a bottle of sparkling water. Uncle had quinine and lime. It had been less than a year since our meeting on the roof in Tel Aviv. Uncle looked just as comfortable here as he did then. His young men were discretely seated a few tables away.

"I'm so glad you could join me, Deck. I'm here to see my nephew and I heard you were in town."

I didn't believe his knowledge of my whereabouts was coincidental.

"It's good to see you, too. I'm afraid it was a bit like the Wild West in New York last year. But all's well that ends well," I added hopefully.

He looked steadily at me without speaking for just a few more tics than were comfortable, but not long enough to be a challenge.

"Yes, it seems there was some high drama and misfortune. But we shall not talk about that again. I am satisfied. In fact, I'd like to discuss another business arrangement."

He turned his attention to our waiter. We both ordered oxtail soup to begin. He chose grilled sea bass with rosemary. I asked for veal steak with morels and spätzle. I suggested Champagne as a compromise that would suit both our dishes. Ruinart Rose is a very good wine but far

The Fall of Declan Curtis

from the excessively expensive bottles which crowded the list. I thought this showed both taste and discretion.

"I don't wish to discuss business while we eat, so allow me to outline my proposition while we wait for our food. This will not involve any danger at all. I am satisfied that you are able to do business effectively and fairly. I would like you to be my selling agent in the US. I will consign shipments to you on a regular basis. Everything will be legal and documented. No drama or gangsters. Just normal trade."

Our soup arrived. I was thankful for the pause. My mind was racing a bit. This could be a significant opportunity: thousands of rugs to sell and no up-front costs. It was a formula for prosperity. If the details could be worked out, the potential was enormous. There simply was no down side. In my business, the stock that did not sell quickly could rapidly tie up capital as it sat dormant. But with everything on consignment, there was no risk for me. I wanted to make this work.

"Well," I said after the soup, "I'm very interested. If we can work out the details, I think I can provide a valuable service to you."

"I know you can, Deck. You won't be surprised that I've learned everything about your business and your business practices. You will be our first associate outside of the family but we are agreed upon it. This will be profitable for us and a great opportunity for you. We'll have no trouble with terms. Your life is about to change."

The champagne was poured before the food arrived. It was ideally chilled. I admired its ruby color as I toasted my new business partner. He drank sparingly as we ate. The food was perfectly prepared. I drank more of the wine than he did, but I was too embarrassed to finish the bottle alone. Alas, sacrifices had to be made.

Chapter Seventeen
The Hotel

THE SWEDE CAME to the Port right out of college. He opened a real estate office on State Street and started to buy residential properties when most homes were selling between ten and twenty thousand dollars. Federal money was pouring into town in the form of Urban Renewal and Historic Preservation grants. The first wave of "renewal" destroyed two thirds of the historic downtown. The second wave preserved enough of the brick commercial district to make the town a magnet for new "settlers" to come and make the Port their home. He was there at just the right moment, but the Swede was undercapitalized and undisciplined. He had a great run for about five years. He sported exotic cars and big mansions and beautiful women, both married and unmarried. When he first got into financial difficulties, several convenient fires kept him afloat for a while. He somehow managed to avoid bankruptcy. But had to give up everything at the end except for the Grand Hotel, a three story brick Federal period architectural gem. It hadn't functioned as a hotel for many decades but the roof still didn't leak. As long as you could keep water and fire out of these old buildings, they would stand forever. He was holed up there without any money for electricity or heat. Some of his Bohemian pals who crashed there painted scenes of people dancing on the inside of the first floor windows. From the outside it seemed as if a Gatsbyesque ball were in full swing. The Swede was trying to hang on until he could find a buyer. It was his last chance to leave town with some capital.

  Uncle's shipments of rugs had been coming in like clockwork. Although I had made a half million dollars in

The Fall of Declan Curtis

1992, it was time to plan new selling and investment strategies. I had been wholesaling mid-range rugs to small and medium size dealers around the country. I saved special pieces in my warehouse. I had plans for a gallery. I planned to mount exhibitions and publish catalogues as I had seen my friends in Europe do. The Grand Hotel would be the perfect venue.

~ ~ ~

"Gus, how are the blueprints for the hotel project coming along?" I asked on the phone.

"That's all I've been doing for weeks. There's an amazing amount of space. There are three thousand feet on the main floor for gallery space. The second floor can be all the storage and office space you need, with a few potential guest rooms as well. And you could live like a prince on the third floor. You probably want to think about an elevator, too."

"The Swede has no phone, so we'll have to go see him tonight and hope he's received my letter with the offer. And even if he's read it, I guess we also have to hope he remembers it."

We parked behind the hotel that night and banged away at the back door for about fifteen minutes. Finally, it opened.

"Oh, I thought I heard something," he said in his heavy accent. The Swede's eyes were bleary and his former sartorial splendor was not even a memory. He wore jeans and a shirt which had once been a preppy statement but was too tattered to matter anymore. The only light in this hall fell from the streetlamp outside. An eerie glow cast flickering shadows from the ballroom at the end of the hall. A dull roar echoed back there as well.

"Come in, let's not stand here in the dark."

We followed him through the gloom into the ballroom. I didn't think this train wreck of a man could shock me, but

John Jeremiah

I was speechless. The source of the flickering light and the ambient roar was a gas pipe. He had cut it half way to the ceiling, bent it about 45 degrees into the room, and lit it. A steady, three foot flame provided a flickering light, and heat, as well as the possibility of immolation.

"You know," Gus said to him, "even if you have insurance, they'll never pay if you burn this dump down."

"Oh, yeah, you're probably right," the Swede mumbled vaguely. "Come on in and sit. I have some weed and some wine."

"And I see we have another guest, as well," I said, as I nodded to the art dealer.

I smirked at Gus. The absurdity was comical. Like the Swede's real estate empire, The Pritchart Gallery had had a great run. In the beginning he had done serious work and even published respectable catalogues and a few academic articles. Pritchart had meticulously restored a Georgian mansion just a block away from the Grand. Along the way, he got into currency trading. I once visited the mansion to look at his rugs. As part of the tour, he took me to the third floor where he had a long bank of computers. This was before many private people had computers. Then he told me about his currency trading. What he didn't mention was that he had been convincing local businessmen to invest in paintings he didn't own. He had even conned some respectable local figures to invest in paintings that were still in museums. He promised ridiculous returns which would have set off alarms with sophisticated investors. This was only made possible by a combination of their greed, provincialism, and his charm. The inevitable end was closing in on him. He was as desperate and delusional as the Swede was now.

"Mr. Pritchart," I said with exaggerated courtesy, "how are you this evening?"

"Checking into the Grand?" Gus cracked before

The Fall of Declan Curtis

Pritchart could answer.

"Fine, I'm fine. Why, no, no. I'm not checking in," he stammered with a watery grin. He looked nervously at the three suitcases he was sitting upon.

The Swede invited us to sit down as well, but left us to scavenge for chairs in order to do so. He gave us glasses of ghastly red wine-like liquid. We thanked him and promptly shelved them.

"Look, I want to be completely honest with you, Deck. Pritchart here is also interested in buying the Grand. I thought it would only be fair if we talked it out together."

One of my Curtis Rules is never to trust anyone who announces he is or wants to be "honest" with you. If honesty is not a given, no pledge will make it so. Of course, neither of these potential jailbirds was to be trusted anyway.

"Well, that's mighty large of you. Let's get right to business then. Pritchart, how much are you willing to pay for the Grand?"

He looked gobsmacked. They were expecting a ritual bargaining dance that would raise the price, I supposed.

"Well, I, I know Swede wants a hundred and eighty thousand."

"It was nice of him to let you know what our deal was, saves me the trouble of telling you myself. Have you got the money?"

"Yes, yes, it's here in cash, a lot of cash. I'll pay two hundred thousand," he added unnecessarily. He patted the suitcases.

"Well, that's fine. You've just bought yourself a hotel. Congratulations. I think we're done here, Gus."

"Wait, Deck, let's be sure this is a real deal," the Swede pleaded. This was not at all what he had hoped for.

"You want to be *sure*? I was sure we had a deal. I came here with a certified check for a hundred and eighty thousand dollars."

John Jeremiah

I took the virginal white draft out of my pocket and let him smell the money as I waved it.

"And you must have been *sure* of Pritchart, since you invited him to bid. So what would you have us do to make sure of him? Shall we have a trial by combat, or shall we perhaps see if he floats in the village pond?"

"That's enough of that. I came here at your invitation, Swede, and in good faith," said Pritchart, sounding a bit huffy.

He leaned over and opened the suitcases. They were jammed with banknotes. They were surprisingly colorful, having come from a dozen different countries. It rather gave the impression of Monopoly money. Obviously, he had bet wrong on some trades and had to take delivery of the currency. This was probably his last fungible asset.

"OK, Pritchart, is that two hundred grand in US dollars?"

"Well, maybe not all of it. I'm not sure. I'll have to figure that out. There's a lot here."

"Well," I said, "is there a hundred and eighty thousand US?"

"I'm just not sure. If it's short, I can get a note for the rest."

"This is your moment of truth, Swede. Are you delusional enough to buy his bullshit? More importantly, do you think I am?"

"No Deck, you're right. We have a deal."

"Wait, I can get you a bond," Pritchart said, "don't throw away twenty grand." His voice trailed off into a whine. I don't think he was really trying to buy The Grand. He had probably been promised a commission by the Swede if he could help boost the price. Now that the Swede had folded, Pritchart would get nothing.

"You know my attorney," I told Swede, " Be there at nine tomorrow morning to sign and get your money. It's too

The Fall of Declan Curtis

late for Pritchart, he's probably going to jail. But you can take this money and start a new life somewhere else before they investigate your old scams. Don't even be fifteen minutes late or you're out of luck. You two have a nice evening. Finish up the wine and weed, just don't be late in the morning."

When we got into the car, I gave Gus two certified checks for twenty thousand each.

"Here, deposit these back into the business account tomorrow."

"Mm, some reinforcements in case you had to bid?"

"Those broken men are like children. This is a big step, Bubba. This building will be 'world headquarters' for the rug enterprise. And when our business days are over and the Port is a big tourist destination, it will be worth millions."

Chapter Eighteen
"Bette Davis Style"

IT TOOK GUS six months to renovate the hotel. We eliminated several interior walls on the first floor. The result was a grand gallery space. We preserved all of the original wainscot, paneled doors, and dentil moldings. That, and the elegant mantels surrounding the Count Rumford fireplaces at either end of the gallery, evoked a refined Federal Period elegance. One could imagine founding fathers congregating in this room to decide the fate of our Republic. My office ran along the back wall of the first floor gallery. The basement proved to be a huge bonus. It was deep and dry. We sandblasted the granite foundation stones. Graceful brick arches supported the four chimneys. Into those we installed racks for wine storage. We built a long mahogany bar and laid a slate floor. This would be a comfortable space for receptions. We stayed with Gus's idea for storage and offices on the second floor. At the East end of the second floor I invited Gus to create a comfortable apartment for himself. This was not entirely selfless on my part. Having him in residence was enhanced security as well as assuring good company. We found a way to fit a decent sized elevator. That made the third floor conveniently accessible. This became my quarters, and a handsome suite it was. We even managed to extend a roof deck around the original cupola. From this perch I had a glorious view of the bay, the barrier island, and the Atlantic Ocean. Life was good.

~ ~ ~

Can you fall in love with a gesture? When I emerged from my office, I saw her at the end of the gallery. Her feet were a little splayed and her head tilted slightly to the right.

The Fall of Declan Curtis

Her hands were tucked into the back pockets of her black silk Capris. Her shiny black hair fell over her left shoulder and splayed across her opalescent silk top. I found that sort of minimalist elegance intoxicating. She was slim and fit and totally unconcerned with the prying eyes of others. She was having a private experience with a glowing Bijar prayer rug. I was alight before I got half way across the floor to her. I suppose if she had turned around and had no teeth, I might have abandoned my quest. But I prefer to think there was some magic that made this inevitable.

"Good evening," I said with forced calmness.

She turned towards my voice and smiled. Her sparkling black eyes seemed receptive to my interruption. She was beautiful in a simple, unglamorous way. I loved her nose first. I'd take my time and love all the rest in due course.

"Hello, is this your gallery?"

"Yes, I'm Declan Curtis, welcome to our first exhibition. Please call me Deck."

"My name is Athena."

"Ah, the virgin goddess of wisdom."

"Well, some wisdom at least. This is an amazing prayer rug."

"Yes, it was made by order of the Shah of Persia in 1850 as a present."

"The colors are so rich, it looks like silk."

"It's just incredibly fine wool pile with a silk foundation. Silk takes up very little room and allows the weaver to tie more knots per square inch. This rug averages six hundred and fifty knots per square inch. It's a masterpiece."

"How do you know about the Shah?"

"It's written in this cartouche. The rest of the writing concerns the thousand names of Allah. But the cartouche tells us he had it made in 1850 for the man who was his finance minister, a famous figure in Persian history. He reorganized their financial system which had completely broken down. You might say he was Persia's Alexander Hamilton."

"Is that why he gave him the rug?"

"In a way it was. He was about to marry the Shah's daughter so the rug may have been a dowry present, although we can't know that."

"Lucky guy."

"Yes and no, the Shah's mother hated her grandson-in-law and was jealous of his power. She had him murdered in a bath house two years later."

"Dangerous part of the world to be in politics."

"Indeed, but it's dangerous here as well."

"Yes, of course."

"May I offer you a drink and a little walk through the collection?"

"That would be lovely."

We settled into my office in comfortable armchairs before a fireplace. I was not at all ashamed of the *cliché*; this was my domain as I would have it. The Italian chairs were upholstered with 17th-century Flemish tapestries, and the carved blue-stone mantel was from the same period. My only concession to practicality was the gas fire. We had decided that wood fires in the gallery space would be too cumbersome, although we used wood on the upper floors. If she was tempted to chide me about my male sanctuary, she hid it well. We agreed on Champagne. I opened a vintage Veuve Cliquot Rose, nice and cold.

"This is an amazing color." she said as she held her crystal flute up to the flickering flames. Of course, she was right. It was a rich ruby red. The intensity of the red varies from vintage to vintage. Sometimes it is a mere blush of pink. This one was particularly deep.

"I must say I enjoy the color as much as the taste, and that's saying quite a lot. Color comes first in the art of carpets. One could spend a lifetime studying dyeing. All

The Fall of Declan Curtis

sorts of plants were used to create color like reds from madder, blues from indigo, and even cochineal purple from worms. And those basic colors were multiplied hundreds of ways by minerals like tin that were added in the mordants. The dyers were the scientists of their day. Renaissance painters crushed precious stones to mix with their pigments to achieve astounding color intensity. I doubt you would even find your food palatable if it were colorless. But enough of my color fetish; please, tell me about yourself."

"I find your fetish fascinating," she said as I filled our flutes again. "I'm an attorney and travel writer."

"Perhaps I will choose not to hear 'attorney' and just focus on travel writer."

"Well, I'm not the kind of attorney most people detest," she said with a forced chuckle. I could see she had tired of this explanation and I regretted making the trite remark. "I do insurance work, specializing in art insurance and recovery."

"I'm sorry, I was glib and that's unattractive. What sort of travel writing have you done?"

"I've written magazine articles about Moscow and several European cities. And I authored a travel guide to the Greek Islands."

"I'll bet the research was enjoyable."

"Yes, it certainly was. I hope to live there for an extended period one day."

"Here's to fulfilled dreams," I toasted. "May I show you around the collection now?"

"Certainly!"

I showed her through some large decorative carpets from the nineteenth century and tried to stay out of the lecture mode. We spoke of color and design theory. When we reached a display of South Persian tribal weavings, she perked up.

"These look like Indian designs."

"Yes, a lot of people say that. The execution of geometrical designs on a grid limits graphic possibilities. There are only so many ways you can describe a circle or a square, although they are quite creative about it. But the limitations of a loom grid results in striking resemblances among weavings from the Middle East to ancient South American cultures. I'll stop now before you slip into a coma."

"No, not at all. It's fascinating. What are all the small things for?"

I showed her saddle bags that served as pillows when not used in moving, small bags the women wove for themselves as purses, and box-shaped weavings used to store bedding.

"They made everything they needed," I said, "utensil holders, salt bags, saddle blankets and decorated ties to fasten their belongings to the animals."

"And it's all so beautiful," she said, "I want to know all about it."

"Well, if you give me a few years of your undivided attention, I'll be glad to teach you."

"You'll have to let me check my schedule. I'll get back to you." She gave me what I chose to interpret as a flirty smile.

"So, what sort of writing are you doing now?"

"I have an idea for a guide book that combines Greek mythology with the islands and temples connected to the ancient stories."

"Sounds interesting. I won't ask you to give anything away, but perhaps you'd be willing to expand on that over dinner sometime soon?"

She hesitated a moment. She dipped her head slightly and looked at me with upturned eyes. I wasn't sure what she was thinking, but her hook was deep in my palate.

"Or anything else you want to talk about would be fine," I added in an attempt to cut off any possible retreat.

The Fall of Declan Curtis

"I'm going back to Manhattan tomorrow. Do you like oysters?"

"Indeed I do, in any of god's manifestations or man's manipulations."

"Ok, Deck, that's the right answer. Can you get away next week?"

"Sure," I said. If she had asked me to meet her in Tunisia tomorrow, I would have been there early.

"All right, I'll meet you Monday night at the Oyster Bar in Grand Central Terminal."

"That's great. It's a nostalgic place for me. My dad used to take me there when I was a boy."

"You ate oysters as a child?"

"No, he did. I ate lemon sole, but I'm on the program now."

"Listen, I do want to get to know you better. But I also have an ulterior motive for being in your gallery. A client of ours had a burglary. You would recognize the family name. Among the lost items were many valuable carpets and tapestries. The company wants to use a firm that is not part of the New York scene."

"I see. Let me tell you right off, accurate appraisals can't be properly done from pictures. But we can establish approximate values. Invoices from their purchases can be useful, too, if they have them."

"No, you don't understand. The thieves are negotiating with our company to return the stolen pieces. The company offered a "finder's fee" and "no questions asked" for the return of the goods. What we need is someone to confirm that these really are the same things that were stolen and that they haven't suffered any damage that will affect their value."

I tried earnestly to focus on her story. But a wave of her hair kept spilling over her left eye like Veronica Lake's. Then I'd resist the urge to reach out and tuck it back behind her ear. I simply didn't know her well enough to touch her like that yet. But I certainly intended to.

"Deck, Deck, are you with me? Am I boring you?"

"Of course not. The job is simple. I was just thinking about where we'll have dinner after our oysters and champagne."

"You're not very serious, are you?"

"About business, no. But when it comes to food, I am deadly serious. As Oscar said, only shallow people take meals lightly."

When she didn't ask "Oscar who?" I was even warmer towards this goddess of wisdom.

"The oyster bar will be our date, but dinner will involve my boss, Bob Dexter. It's only a formality, but he'll have to approve your hiring. My conscience is clear now that I've explained the reason for my visit. I was not expecting to be charmed, as well. Shall we say seven o'clock?"

She reached out for my hand as she stood. She sandwiched my hand between both of hers. With a confident tilt towards me, she bussed me on the cheek and whispered "Thanks" in my ear. I felt like I just got a date to the prom.

Chapter Nineteen
Athena

ATHENA LEFT THE GRAND HOTEL and entered the neat little park that featured a bronze statue of William Lloyd Garrison, The Great Liberator. He lived here in the Port while running his abolitionist campaign. The palpable history of this old Colonial city enchanted her. She wandered down the main commercial street and spent some time admiring the Universalist Church, a two-hundred year old wedding cake of a structure wrought in the purest classical style to be found in New England. She slipped into a quiet tavern and compromised with a mediocre glass of Pinot Gris. She was unsettled. She could have stayed longer at the gallery or gone to dinner with Deck, but she wanted to shake his spell. She felt just slightly threatened by her response to him.

The visit had certainly been pleasant. He had nice hands and a confident worldliness that she found attractive. She'd been divorced for a few years now. She'd been on a hundred first dates without feeling inspired by any of them. Her ex was a scientist who was worldly in his own way, and very intelligent. But his was an internal life with little to share. What had begun as a great adventure, devolved into dual existences and mutual resentments. In the end, it was his unfaithfulness that brought things to a conclusion. Since then she had formed an international life style based on her interest in classical Greece and supported by a wide array of friends from around the world. She had learned to be single and liked it.

Joan had dropped Athena off at the gallery. Athena used the payphone to call her friend and hostess for a ride back to the house. Joan was a college friend who had invited her to visit while she was in the Port. The two women had fallen into the old habits of their friendship, as if the decade had had simply been a vacation. Athena smiled as she watched her friend enter and wave to some people she knew with small-town ease. Her old roommate was trim and it occurred to Athena that she could wear the same clothes they had worn ten years ago.

"How was the gallery?" Joan asked when she sat down.

"Very impressive. They have something special going on there. It seems odd to find that sort of sophistication in this backwater."

Joan quietly surveyed the elegant simplicity of her friend's outfit. Athena had an air of urbanity that was slightly out of place in this informal seaport. No one would have mistaken her for a native.

"Hey, that's my home town you are having fun with. This "backwater" has been producing pirates, politicians, writers, artists and oddballs of all types for hundreds of years. So, a little respect, please."

They both laughed and ordered another round.

"So, did you hire someone to do the insurance appraisal?"

"Yes, indeed. The owner himself is coming down to the city next week. He's interesting."

"Oh, really," Joan said with an exaggerated drawl.

"Alright, calm down. It's not a big deal but I have to admit he was more interesting than the empty suits I meet in the insurance business."

"Do tell."

"Well, I'm not sure where to start. He's a few years older. He knows his field and he has a way of making you comfortable while he lectures. Most men can't stay charming while showing off."

John Jeremiah

"Tell me about it! How is he in the looks department?"

"He's fine, good looking but not a pretty boy. He's well dressed, but not a dandy. I think he has his clothes made."

"Why didn't I go with you and why didn't I meet him first?"

"Seems to me, you have one at home already."

"Details, details. So what's next?"

"Aside from a business dinner to introduce him to my boss, who knows?"

As they drove towards the ocean at the Port's South End, the sun was throwing its last fiery rays up behind them. This low area by the bay was the oldest part of town. The local name for the neighborhood was Joppa Flats. The real old-timers called it "Joppy." Joan and her husband were fortunate to own a saltbox on Neptune Street that dated to the 1650s. The building was framed in oak and chestnut. The beams and the low wooden ceilings were unpainted. They had mellowed to a deep cordovan brown. The floors were wide, first growth pine that had a scoured silvery-blonde surface that had never been painted. The dark wood sucked up the light. There were a few narrow casement windows with diamond pane leaded glass. It would have been gloomy but for the warm glow of the fireplace. That was ten feet wide and five feet tall. A mammoth oak beam supported the masonry above the firebox. At the rear wall of the firebox was a brick oven for cooking. The girls settled in with drinks before the fire. Being there was a time-travel experience.

"How was the exhibition downtown?" Jim asked when he finally sat down with his own drink.

"It was very interesting. They did a great job on the old hotel. He has an elegant gallery on the first floor. They made a big wine cellar and pub atmosphere down there as well."

"Yes, I've seen Curtis around town for years. I never

got to know him but his star certainly seems to be rising."

"She's being coy, Jim. It turns out that he's a lady killer."

"That's not true Joan. You always look for drama. I was only with him for two hours."

"Just long enough to hire him to go down to the city next week. And to dinner," Joan said with a rising inflection in her teasing way.

Tonight's dinner was a lobster spectacular. The "walk in" fireplace was not only the social focus of Joan's home, it was a major source of heat and a chance to do dramatic cooking. The beehive-shaped ovens in the back of the fire wall could be heated with shoveled coals and used for baking. The original iron bars remained in the throat of the chimney. From these, hooked chains were hung and a huge kettle could be suspended over the fire. Joan made a big production of pouring six bottles of cheap champagne and a six-pack of Bass Ale into the cauldron. As that concoction came to a boil, they chanted "bubble, bubble, toil and trouble" as they giggled and dropped in half a dozen pound and a quarter lobsters to steam away.

Athena and Joan had begun to take cooking seriously when they had an apartment together at college. Their kitchen became a social center. Eating a mess of lobsters was a quintessential New England experience. An Alsatian Pinot Blanc accompanied the fare. Joan must have remembered Athena's passion from school because she finished with a Tarte Tatin, a desert her guest would have committed sin for when they were young. Afterwards, Athena made a perfunctory offer to help clean up but her hosts told her to relax.

She excused herself and took a walk to the seawall. The house was only about fifty yards from the bay. She sat on the seawall and looked across the water. It was perfectly still. At the far end of the bay, the mouth of the river was a

John Jeremiah

narrow and treacherous channel separating the north shore from the sandy barrier beach island that protected the bay from the ocean. Ancient oyster middens were found on the island in the seventeenth century. The local tribes had celebrated on the beach for hundreds of years and left mountains of shells. When the English settled here in 1635, lobsters were so prolific that they crawled out of the water and could be had by simply picking them up from the sand. They were not considered fit food and were served to prisoners. The warm memory of the sweet lobster meat made her smile. How could anyone think lobster was junk food? Of course, these same folks thought tomatoes were poisonous. A nearly full moon was rising over the island and reflecting on the water.

Athena couldn't define her feelings about this new man. She was interested but calm and detached. This wasn't one of those high octane infatuations that could seize your mind and quickly burn itself out. And yet, there was some power to her feelings. She liked the timbre of his voice. His touch on her arm was reassuring. She wanted to know more about him.

Chapter Twenty
Kissing the Ocean

LEAVING THE GALLERY only a few days after our grand opening was not wise. Taking a foolish insurance job was a waste of time. But I wanted to waste a lot of time with her. Athena made me want to do foolish things. And if owning your own enterprise didn't allow you waste a little time, what was the point of having it? Fortunately, I had an excellent staff that could manage while I was away for a few days. I could check in daily, and in the worst case, I was only a few hours away.

I took the train from South Station that Monday. It was slower than the plane but I found it more relaxing. Perhaps I had a greater appreciation for this form of travel from my time in Europe. Of course, the comfort level of Euro trains was vastly superior. Nonetheless, the unhurried pace was alluring. Being out of reach had its charm. And the train, with one transfer, would plant me right in Grand Central. That would make up some time versus flying. I enjoyed the room and the option to walk around and even to visit the bar. I had a suitcase and I didn't have to worry about airport security. So, although I doubted I would need it, I had packed my Walther. Even cooperative criminals who wanted to make a deal could be unpredictable.

The rhythm lulled me. I thought about taking that ride only a few years before to my dad's funeral. I composed his eulogy on the way down on scraps of paper and cocktail napkins. In spite of this improvisation, it was well received by the hundreds of people who showed up at the service. Besides swathes of family and college friends, the church was filled with various ranks of police, FBI, and politicians.

After changing trains at Penn Station, I got to Grand

The Fall of Declan Curtis

Central Terminal an hour early. That gave me plenty of time to walk over to the Waldorf and leave my bag. In spite of some of the ugly glass International style buildings that were built thirty years before, the view uptown was still timeless. And the view of the Terminal still stirred me. This was the heart of "public" Manhattan for me, along with the Chrysler Building and a few other monumental works. It was hard to imagine that the barbarians had tried to demolish it as they did Pennsylvania Station. I always fall into a dream state when I enter the main lobby. The scale is Olympian and the vaulted ceiling sports a classical starscape replete with the Zodiac. The energy of the crowd is palpable. In this secular temple of the New World, one can believe in permanence and lofty civilization, if only for a moment.

Slipping down the ramps under the main floor I recalled the many lunches I had at the Oyster Bar with my dad. Endless racks of oysters from every bay and inlet from Prince Edward Island to the Chesapeake were stacked on ice behind the long bar. The double vaulted ceilings were tiled with patterns that fascinated me as a boy. With all of these nostalgic thoughts occupying my mind, I headed through the swinging doors at the end of the bar and into the "saloon" where I was to meet Athena. She was comfortably seated with a glass of white wine.

She was like still water in the midst of rapids, perfectly composed and untouched by the hullabaloo around her. She looked up and smiled.

"I know I'm not late, so that makes you early," I said with a stupid grin.

"Well, you got me there, buster. I live pretty close by and it was easy to walk over. If you prefer, I could slip out and make you wait twenty minutes."

"And waste our time alone before our business meeting? Not a chance."

John Jeremiah

I chose a crisp Heidsieck Monopole champagne to complement our Malpeque oysters from Prince Edward Island. While I like many different types of oysters, these extreme Northern bivalves have a clean, fresh flavor that is pleasing to me. Their brine is balanced with sweetness.

"Deck, these are the perfect size, temperature, and flavor. I'm afraid we'll have to order more."

"You remind me of the French poet who said 'eating oysters is like kissing the ocean on the lips'," I said.

I don't know how she managed to do it so gracefully, but Athena rose slightly and gave me a light kiss on the lips. The gesture was effortless and largely unnoticed by others.

"Now eating oysters will remind me of kissing you on the lips." She slapped me with a devastating smile.

I've known many types of women, from femme fatales to fresh country girls. She has it all covered. I couldn't get enough of her. I hated to leave for our meeting. I wanted her to myself.

"Well, I suppose we should get a check and go meet Bob," she said.

"Let me," she began as I reached for the check.

"That's all right, I'll be billing your bosses quite enough to keep us in oysters and champagne for a while."

~ ~ ~

We met Mr. Dexter at the 21 Club. While still a charming and quirky New York institution, you were more likely to rub elbows with business people than celebrities or high society types. It seemed to me a perfect choice for the mid-level exec. After perfunctory introductions at the bar, we headed to our table in the back. The room had been accumulating toys and sports memorabilia for generations. They were hung from the ceiling. The effect always struck me as odd, like a high class sports bar.

"Bob, this is Declan Curtis, our oriental rug expert," she continued as we shook hands, "and this is Bob Dexter, our

The Fall of Declan Curtis

vice president of claims."

We invited each other to use our first names.

Bob was well turned out. The suit was nicely tailored with details I liked. Hand-done top stitching graced properly proportioned lapels. His tie featured an elegant double Windsor knot, the dimple dead center. I hadn't seen one so perfect since Ronnie Reagan or Fritz Mondale. His nails were manicured and buffed but without a gaudy shine. His hair was blond and abundant, carefully swept to one side. He spoke with a smiling sincerity. I felt as if I were being coaxed to like him.

But I didn't.

Bob and I had perfect medium rare sirloins and Athena had some sort of salad. He was indifferent about the wine so I had my own way with it.

"I'm not trying to put myself out of work here, but why don't you just go to the police?'

"Of course, police reports were duly filed. But it's simply a business calculation, Deck. If we don't get the property back, we'll have to pay over a million dollars replacement value. These thieves will sell it all back to us for two hundred thousand. If we can make the client whole and cut our loss by eighty percent, it only makes sense to do so."

"Have you done this sort of thing before?" I asked.

"Yes, not often, but we've saved a lot of money in the past with this method. Of course, we have to make sure we aren't scammed. It's my neck on the line when I OK this sort of deal. If it goes south for any reason, I'm fired. That's why I need you to verify the property."

"What about security? Are you doing anything to protect yourself from being mugged for the money?"

"Yes, when you inspect the property, we will have no money with us. Once you have verified, we'll lock and seal the truck. They will drive it to our warehouse in Long Island City. The money will be passed out to them through a bullet proof turnstile after the truck is safely inside."

"Well, that's not exactly fool-proof, Bob."

"Of course not, but a certain amount of mutual trust is involved in all these situations. There is no reason for anyone to get hurt. It's a win-win situation for everybody as long as no one panics."

"Why not just have them all arrested when they show up for the inspection?"

"Deck, I'm willing to pay you well to do a simple job. I don't need a general." There was an edge to his voice which belied his calm demeanor. "I just need a lieutenant. But if you must know, we'd never be able to do this sort of money-saving deal again if word got out that we double-crossed them."

"All right, Bob, you're the boss. But if I'm going into a warehouse with a crew of professional thieves and only you for protection, it's going to cost you ten grand."

"That's fine. Athena will be there as our lawyer and witness."

"Not on your life. We go alone."

"Deck, you don't understand, this is part of my job," Athena said, "why would they hurt us? We won't have any money. All they want is a clean exchange. They're professionals."

"I've already had some experience in this area. There are a million things that can go wrong when you're dealing with crooks. You're not dealing with a team of lawyers who have decided what's in their best interest. It's usually a group of low IQ thugs working for a couple of wise guys who aren't always in control of their soldiers. In fact, some of the smartest bosses wind up getting buried by their dummies."

"Deck, you can't tell me what my job is." Athena's eyes grew steely. "This is the plan, take it or leave it. You're not my daddy."

I've got to say, I didn't like this at all. I didn't like Bob. I

The Fall of Declan Curtis

didn't like his creepy smile. And I didn't like his naive plan. I kept thinking about the "simple" hand-off in Red Hook that ultimately resulted in six deaths. I thought I had left all that behind me. No, I didn't like this at all. And I would have walked away if not for Athena. My Walther and I would be there to make sure she got out OK. But as far as I was concerned, Bob was on his own.

~ ~ ~

Athena and I met for breakfast at Les Halles down on Park Avenue South. It's an authentic French bistro. We had French press coffee, strong and black. The orange juice was fresh-squeezed and the bacon was very smoky. Poached eggs and a platter of breads and pastries rounded out our order. I told her about the trouble I'd had with a previous hand-off. I didn't get into the bloodshed, and I changed the locale of the story. But I wanted to demonstrate how things can go sideways even when there is no good reason for it.

"I appreciate your concern, Deck. But you must realize I've been in the rodeo for a while myself. Let's get this thing done and move on."

"Move on to us?"

She held my gaze for what seemed like a long time.

"Yes, I think so. I think we need to find out how we fit."

That was fine with me. We were to join Bob at six in a bar on Third Avenue. We'd get a call telling us where the meeting was. It would be in Manhattan. After the inspection and sealing, they would drive the truck to Long Island City. The truck would be locked in the insurance company's warehouse. Then the payoff would be made.

"I'm looking forward to the fitting, Athena. Meanwhile, I have some business in town. I'll see you at O'Neill's a little before six."

"I have some chores, too. But now I'm going to get a steam bath and full body massage at my gym. I'll have a blissful hour or two of complete relaxation."

"You make it sound like sex."

"It is, a little, but sex doesn't help the pain I have behind my knee from running."

"Clearly, you're doing it wrong," I suggested.

"The massage or the sex?"

"I volunteer to help with either."

She looked up at me and shook her head a bit.

"See you tonight, smart ass."

~ ~ ~

I'd called Red before I came down from Boston. I told him this was just insurance company business but I'd fill him in when I knew more. This time I had to meet him at the precinct instead of at a bar. I gave him the run down.

"So, the greedy bastards want to steal from each other, let 'em."

"That's mighty broadminded of you, Red."

He just chuckled.

"Here's what I have in mind. What do you say you give me a couple of trackers? I can plant them deep inside the rugs as we roll them up. The truck then has a long drive to the insurance warehouse. You can have them stopped for a tail light or something. They won't even know they've been double crossed. The insurance company won't have to pay anything. And some of your boys will get a high profile collar. What's wrong with that?"

"Like everything else we do, we won't know what's wrong with it until it happens, boyo. But I have to say it sounds good. Sit here while I run it by the Captain."

Well, the Captain went with the plan. It didn't require the cavalry, just a squad car or two and a few trackers. It was a small price for a potential "million dollar" coup and all the attendant publicity.

"Now Red, it's important that we make this a routine traffic stop. I don't want the insurance company mad at me. I might get some more of this easy money down the line."

The Fall of Declan Curtis

"You just watch out for yourself, Deck. Don't take any chances. We'll always be close to the trackers. We'll know when you make the first stop. When the trackers take off again, we'll know you're clear and the rabbit is fair game."

Even I was starting to feel that this would work. I got to O'Neill's and realized I was the first one to the party. I ordered a pint of Guinness and a bump of Jameson's. I started to brood a bit. I figured I'd have my jacket off while I crawled about the rugs. That eliminated shoulder or waistband carry. So, I wore baggy trousers. My Walther was in an ankle holster. I knew in my heart that I would kill anyone who threatened her. What the hell else could I do?

Athena was next to arrive. She was in slacks and flats.

"Good," I said eying her shoes, "I've seen too many women fall on heels and get eaten by the monster."

"Nobody's getting eaten tonight, soldier. This is strictly business."

"From your lips to god's ear. There's only one thing worrying me."

"What's that?" she said.

"I finally figured out who Dexter reminds me of."

"OK, I'll bite."

"Dan Duryea. Remember him? Always looked good in an oily sort of way. But he was always the bad guy, either right off or in the end. Bad news."

Athena laughed.

"Now that you say it I can see it, especially the hair. But that's a hell of a way to make judgments about people, by what fictional character they remind you of."

I smirked as Dan Duryea walked in and joined us.

"Hello Bob, heard anything yet?"

"Yes, that's why I'm late. They called the office," he began. I didn't like the way he avoided my eyes as he rushed through his lines. "we'll take a cab to 114th street. I have the lock and seal in this briefcase. When we're done, we'll take

John Jeremiah

a cab back down here."

The gang was there before us. Two of them loitered on the street on either side of a corrugated steel overhead door. After our cab left, one of them gave a four knock rap on the door. Immediately it started to rumble up. A fairly new and clean box truck was visible. Three more hoods stood by it.

"Hello folks. I'm Sal. Let's keep this friendly and fast. Got your inventory list?"

As Bob started to open his brief case, Sal grabbed it and carelessly dumped it on the floor.

"What'd you think he had in there, a tommy gun?" I opined. "He's just a suit, not a superhero."

This guy was cool and not to be thrown off his game.

"And who are you, wise guy?"

"I'm even less of a threat. I'm an antiques dealer, here to vet the goods. And let's not have any jokes about my loafers," I hitched a thumb towards Athena, "but you want to keep an eye on her, though. She's a lawyer."

"OK, Dangerfield, let's get the show on the road."

Bob picked up his inventory list from the floor and we climbed into the truck. I showed them which carpets I needed to see unrolled on the floor. While they opened them, I inspected many of the small pieces right in the truck. While I was at it, I planted the two bugs in them. We wrapped up the big carpets and balanced out the inventory against the goods. There were a few small things missing. But we had more than ninety percent of the haul and it was in perfect condition. The whole process took just over an hour. Then Bob sealed the door latch with a lock and the lead disc. We thought we were done. I was feeling pretty good about the tenor of the situation. None of the goons even spoke to us except for Sal.

"OK, you two, get out of here," he said to Athena and me.

"Your money is waiting for you at the warehouse," Bob

The Fall of Declan Curtis

said with a slight quaver in his voice.

"You're coming with us, pal," Sal told Bob as two goons grabbed him by the shoulders. Athena looked to me for some guidance.

"You kids want to come for a ride, too?" Sal asked.

Bob looked at me pleadingly. I didn't hesitate. You know how I feel about him.

"No thanks, I'm just going to rustle up a cab. Good evening to you."

Sal called after us, "Bob will be home later, as long as everything goes as planned. Don't do anything to spoil the party."

Well, I told you right from the beginning that Bob was on his own. I really felt that if this were the only glitch in the plan, we had done pretty well for ourselves. Maybe I felt a little guilty about the hazard Bob would be in when the truck got pulled over. But I had to trust to fate and New York's finest that no one would be shot in the process.

"Do you think everything will be all right?"

"Everything is all right. You and I are free, your company owes me ten grand, and we are going to find out how we fit. I'd say 'god's in his heaven, all's right with the world'."

"You know what I mean," she could not entirely hide a smirk, "is Bob going to be all right?"

"Why not? As long as the money is there at the warehouse, everything should be peachy."

So, I was not entirely forthright. But we would learn everyone's fate when the morning newspapers arrived at my suite in the Waldorf. Meanwhile, I was sure that any sleep we lost would not be over Bob.

Chapter Twenty-One
The Morning After

I SUPPOSE it would be unnatural of me not to think of Anne that night. After all, Athena was the first woman I had slept with since Anne ran off with Gator. That was four years ago now. I hoped Anne had a great time with him because our sex life was nothing special. Everyone deserves to have a real wrestling match before they get too old for the action. My night with Athena was special. Part of it may have been the excitement of being in personal danger. The adrenaline rush got me in the right mood for sex. I remember having a frightening accident driving a friend's Morgan when I was in college. My girlfriend and I were shaken up but uninjured. We made a bee-line for my friend's apartment and put rabbits to shame until we ultimately passed out. It was a more mature fury with which Athena and I coupled that night. We fit just fine, and often.

The phone woke us at eight. It was Bob.

"I've been trying to get Athena. Do you have any idea where she could be?"

"No, Bob, I don't. But I can help you. I'm meeting her for brunch in the Palm Court at the Plaza. You sound like you need to pee. What's the problem?"

"We got pulled over by the police, something about a tail light. Then everything went crazy. Of course, they had no manifest for the freight when the police opened the truck. I thought I was going to be shot. Both of the drivers had guns and the police were extremely nervous. Eventually, I convinced them that I was a victim and not a perpetrator. I don't know what's going to happen now."

"I imagine you will need a serious defense attorney. I

The Fall of Declan Curtis

doubt you'll be charged with anything, but you'll want your interests looked after in any case. Perhaps you should start by talking to Athena? Why don't you calm down and meet us at the Plaza at ten?"

As she listened, Athena looked concerned and amused at the same time. I winked at her.

She ran her hand over my bicep after I hung up.

"I wouldn't have guessed you were a tattooed man."

"That's a bit of a story. Somewhat ill-considered, I suppose. But it was my first and probably my last."

"Are you going to tell me about it?'

"I did that when I was feeling very much in tune with Robert Johnson. I'll tell you the story when there's time. We need to go soon."

I plumped two pillows up and prepared to watch her get out of bed and off to the shower. I hadn't really gotten a look at her in the dark, and I relished seeing her lovely body in daylight. I leaned back and opened a bottle of seltzer.

"I'll let you go first. Everything you need in toiletries is in there, but I can't help you with clothes."

She hopped off the side of the bed and tried to pull a top sheet with her. I held on to the other end.

"Oh, so you're a voyeur."

"Not at all, my dear, I'm a connoisseur of beauty and I see you as all of the three graces in one."

She let her half of the sheet drop. She locked my eyes in an intense stare, as if daring me to look down at her body, uninvited. After a few moments, she smiled and turned away. Hers was a slim and lithe body and it swayed like the life-force itself. I had to restrain myself from leaping after her. My god, what had I done?

Athena insisted on a brief stop at her apartment for a costume change. We beat Bob to the Plaza, which was just as well since we didn't want to be seen walking in together. No need for him to know anything about us. The Palm Court was my favorite breakfast spot in the city. It's an over-the-top Beaux-Arts confection with a stained glass ceiling and lovely light. The fresh squeezed orange juice was superb, albeit priced like an entry-level champagne. We settled on that with coffee and croissants while we waited for Bob.

"What do you think happened?" she asked.

"He was pretty direct. They had some sort of traffic stop and everything unraveled. No one got hurt."

Athena had just begun to speculate about the ramifications with management when Bob stumbled in. He had clearly not taken my advice to calm down. Neither had he shared Athena's prudence in the form of a costume change, or a bath for that matter. He rather reminded me of Joel Cairo, disheveled in the Fairmount lobby after being grilled all night.

"Where have you been?" he snapped at Athena. His petulance annoyed me.

"Sit down, Bob." I said, "Try to relax. Have some coffee or orange juice. Just tell us what happened."

"You don't understand. This is awful. I could have been shot," his voice rose with a crackle.

"Look Bob, if you are going to act like an hysterical woman, I'm going to have to slap you."

Bob looked at me as if he were seeing me for the first time. I leaned towards him until we were *tête-à-tête*.

"Think carefully before you begin Bob. Let's have a nice breakfast and a simple account of the proceedings."

Bob cleared his throat a few times. He took a long draft of orange juice. He played with his cutlery and took a deep breath.

"Alright, I'm sorry. I'm not used to being in the middle of a raid. The truck was only about twenty minutes away from where we left you when a squad car flashed its lights at us. The two men who took me discussed what they would do."

Bob seemed to calm down as he got into his report. He even buttered a croissant as he spoke.

"Anyway, they concluded that the truck was too awkward for an escape. So, cooperation was the plan. They played along with the traffic ticket until the cops insisted on looking inside. Then they immediately surrendered their weapons and asked for lawyers. Maybe I exaggerated the danger but several more squad cars showed up within minutes. There were lots of drawn weapons. Anything could have happened."

"Now don't get yourself worked up again, Bob. It seems to me that this is a perfect solution for your employers. Except for my ten thousand, you have recovered the loss in perfect condition without paying a dime. As Dr. Pangloss would say, 'everything is for the best in this best of all possible worlds!'"

Bob looked at me as if he were only understanding every other word.

"Yes, I suppose you are right," he said vaguely. "What do you think of this, Athena?"

"Look, Deck's right. But we should get to the boss's office right away and paint this all a happy color. If we control the narrative from the start, we'll come out looking good. The result will overshadow any impetuosity on our part."

"Bob, I suggest you go straight to your apartment and clean up. You can meet Athena at the office in an hour and start 'controlling your narrative'."

I couldn't resist satirizing her jargon.

He looked at Athena and she gave him a silent nod.

"See you then," he said to her. He had no salutation for me. I suspect he had begun to appreciate my disdain for him. Off he scampered, like a man who wanted to leave before the waiter discovered he hadn't left a tip.

"What's your take on this," I asked Athena, "He seems

unduly upset to me."

"Well, he's obviously not a brave sort. I doubt he's ever even seen someone pull a gun before."

"I still think he's overreacting. Anyway, I don't care. Look, I have ten grand that I'm not doing anything with. I've got to go to Switzerland tomorrow. I'll be done with business in a few days. Why don't you meet me in Paris?"

Her eyes arched a bit. She examined her place setting intensely. Then she looked up at me.

"Are we getting ahead of ourselves?" she said softly.

"It's only geography. If we don't do that we'll just spend a lot of time together here in New York. Now, I've nothing against that either. New York is grand and you're the only person I want to think about right now. But Paris is Elysium. It's not my city or your city, it's neutral ground for lovers. And the food is pretty good, too."

She still hesitated.

"Look, I'll send you plane tickets and hotel reservations from Zurich. If you decide you don't want to come, just cash them in and buy yourself a motorcycle. No hard feelings."

"Deck, you're a hard man to say no to. But let me make myself clear, I don't want to say no. But I'm not promising anything either. Let's play and see where it goes. And 'no hard feelings' if it doesn't work."

"OK, sister, you've got a date. By the way, I need your details for the airline tickets."

We finished our brunch of Eggs Benedict with a crisp Prosecco. I took her arm as we left the table.

"See if you can keep Bob from throwing up on his tie while you explain things to your boss."

We were on the steps outside the Plaza. She turned to answer my wise crack but I gave her a firm but polite kiss on her lovely lips. There was nothing left to say.

"Watch your mail," I said over my shoulder.

Chapter Twenty-Two
Corruption

THE PILOT ANNOUNCED that we would be landing in Zurich in twenty-five minutes. I didn't really need to see Magdi about rugs now that I had Uncle as a prolific source. I guess it was partly my natural inclination to stay diversified. But my foolish loyalty, my almost obsessive responsibility towards anyone who had ever helped me, drove me to answer his call to come and buy some rugs. Anyway, I liked him. I had learned things from him.

We first met in the early 1980s. I was at a small estate auctioneer's gallery in Cambridge. A seemingly hapless Egyptian fellow had found his way to Boston. The rug buyers at the auction would "pool" together to buy the rugs rather than bid against each other. This was a tradition which dated to eighteenth century England. When a stranger showed up expressing interest in the rugs he was ignored. However, I was curious and chatted him up. I wound up taking him back to the Port and hearing his story. I always remember that first visit. As Magdi walked around our narrow colonial streets, he said:

"I can't believe I'm in a real American village!"

As our business relationship grew, I spent several months in Europe each year. His operation in Zurich consisted of a workshop and office on the first floor and living quarters above. This served as our headquarters. In the beginning, I stayed in his guest bedroom. There were twin beds. The remaining small space was stacked with the detritus of centuries, reflecting his other enterprises. On one visit, one twin bed hosted a painted wooden sarcophagus of the fifth dynasty. It was *sans* mummy, to my relief, but still entered my dreams. There were assortments

The Fall of Declan Curtis

of Coptic textile fragments, ancient carnelian beads and bits of Ptolemaic pottery that Bedouins traded, and crates of brown Etruscan pottery figures. The range of items stretched from the ambiguous to the clearly illegal.

On one visit some investigators from Interpol showed up. Evidently, an antiquities dealer in Paris was in a jam about a large granite sculpture she had on display. It belonged in Egypt. They seemed to think that Magdi had some part in facilitating its export in a crate marked as jet engine parts. I didn't ask. Fortunately, they did not have enough proof to detain him. After this, however, I decided that separate quarters would be prudent. This was a sticky situation since it contradicted Magdi's eastern sense of hospitality. In the end, I prevailed but I always felt it had somewhat damaged our relationship.

~ ~ ~

"Your English is very rich," he said to me once.

He was learning at all times. I was a stranger to a relaxed or unguarded Magdi. He seemed so modern and worldly most of time that it always shocked me when some cultural provincialism cropped up. One summer afternoon we had taken a ferry across the lake and enjoyed a tram ride up the side of a mountain. There were two giggly American college girls in our wooden tram. They had loose sweatshirts with school logos. They were hanging all over each other like puppies and whispering secrets to each other. They were completely unselfconscious. I thought Magdi had said "What peaches!" Of course, such an American colloquialism would have been out of place from him.

"Yes, they are lovely." I said with a broad smile.

Magdi frowned, and enunciated "bitches."

"Why are you saying that?"

"They are prostitutes; look at the way they behave."

"Boy, you're all wrong about that. They're just

schoolgirls on vacation."

He looked at me as if I were hopelessly naïve.

~ ~ ~

There was a restaurant at the top of the mountain with a wide outdoor deck and astounding views. I suspected that there was a similar facility on all the mountains in Switzerland. I knew that he was meeting someone but nothing more. Magdi introduced me to Herr Professor Berg, a slightly preposterous man who bore an uncanny resemblance to Martin Heidegger. He was meticulously dressed in English tweeds. He sported an ascot and a fluffed pocket square. But the absence of a pince-nez disappointed me. Although Magdi doesn't drink, we ordered a Premier Cru Chablis. We enjoyed a full lunch with pork medallions and white asparagus. I noticed Herr Professor pocket an envelope that Magdi set on the table.

"Professor Berg is the head of the school where Ali studies."

Now, Ali was a wiry boy from a rural village in Egypt. He repaired rugs in Magdi's unlicensed workshop. A student visa may have gotten him into Switzerland, but I knew for a fact that he had no time to be off to a school.

"That's very interesting," I said, enjoying some mischief. "He's a very diligent young man. How is he doing in his classes? What seems to be his favorite subject?"

Magdi began to squirm but the Professor brightened up and spoke at length about Ali's progress. I realized that this corrupt fool had never met Ali. He was simply taking bribes from Magdi to certify Ali's student visa. I didn't understand his insistence on this charade. It was as if he thought we might be wearing a wire and he needed to confirm his story. Why couldn't he just get a wad of cash in a greasy envelope like any normal grifter? No, he needed to maintain his "dignity" by going through the motions. Our lunch was done. He took his leave with a formal handshake for each

The Fall of Declan Curtis

of us. Once again, he let me down when he omitted a heel-click with his bow.

"He always insists on a fine meal when I pay him," Magdi said glumly.

~ ~ ~

For foreigners and immigrants working on the edge of legality, being pressed for bribes was a constant. Inspectors who came to the workshop to check on workers would step into Magdi's office and leave with a little something. There was a customs inspector who would occasionally demand that we give him a rug from our shipments, despite the fact that our imports were completely legal. But it was better to give than draw unwanted attention. It was all a bit appalling to my young sensibilities at the time. I couldn't possibly guess what crimes were in my future.

~ ~ ~

We had a nickname for Ali. Despite speaking rough versions of Arabic, French, and German, Ali did not speak English at all. This severely limited my communications with him, but we liked each other. He had a habit of answering any question with an ungrammatical "Me? No." In Arabic that was *"ana, la"*. And so, "Anala" became our nonsense nickname for him. I bought a tee shirt from one of the tourist shops at home. I had them embroider the Arabic letters which Magdi had carefully drawn for me, *"Ana, la"*. Ali was thrilled with it. I once asked Magdi why I never saw him wearing it.

"You don't understand. It's precious to him, a special thing made for him in America. He will never wear it. But he might show it to his friends and tell them he has a rich friend in America."

Another time I was rattling on about my plans and told Magdi what I would do "if I were a rich man."

"Deck, you are a rich man."

He told me a story about Ali's trip back to his village in

John Jeremiah

Egypt. He had saved a thousand dollars. He was anxious to show his family that he had achieved success. He brought each of them presents. He gave his father a few hundred dollars, more than the man had ever had at one time. His family had a big dinner for him the first night. In the morning he discovered they had robbed him of his money and his watch. When he confronted them, they threw him out of the house. Ali somehow managed to reach Magdi's mother on a telephone. She got him out of there and back to Zurich.

"I know you think of yourself as a man of the world, Deck, but you have a lot to learn about poverty and riches."

~ ~ ~

I admired the determination and resilience of these people who dared to go to foreign lands and try their luck in the world. A company in Switzerland required the owner to be a Swiss citizen. So, in his first year there, Magdi found a man willing to be the titular head of the company in exchange for being on the payroll in a small way. One morning, after seven or eight months, Magdi found the business account drained. The "president" had absconded with everything. Magdi sold a few things at a loss to raise some capital and simply started over. Some years later we ran into that thief in Berne as he was boarding a plane to Spain.

"You stole my money," Magdi said, *sotto voce*, to him.

"It was my company," he sneered at Magdi as if he were a beggar, "I'll spend the money as I will!"

Again, this ludicrous assumption of dignity before people who knew he was a common thief infuriated me. I wanted to pummel him. But the crime was unprovable without self-incrimination, and years old at that. And we were in an airport where violence would trigger all sorts of unpleasantness. And so, Magdi prudently walked away. He had at least his dignity.

The Fall of Declan Curtis

~ ~ ~

Ten years later, I certainly knew much more about life, and money, and poverty. I had experienced betrayal by a lover and a close friend. I had resorted to violence, even homicide to protect myself, my friends, and my enterprise. The distance between Philip Marlowe and Harry Lime was sometimes blurred. Of course, each decision I had made seemed quite solid in and of itself. But the accumulation of extreme measures gathered a moral weight that exceeded the sum of my individual sins. And once this path was taken, many others were closed forever.

~ ~ ~

Magdi met me at the airport. He was clearly anxious to get me to his workshop. As we drove home he asked me for details about the new gallery.

"Yes," I told him, "it really is a two hundred year old hotel on a beautiful square with a garden in it. I have pictures and architect's blueprints in my suitcase to show you."

"This is wonderful, Deck. It must be very expensive to do. Will people come?"

"Well, I'm betting they will. And I'm going to produce regular catalogues like our friend in Germany. That will bring a lot of international business as well."

"I have something special for you," he said without qualification. And, indeed, he did. It was an antique Persian Bakhtiyari carpet with an intricate tile design in at least fifteen colors. At one end of the carpet was a red ground cartouche with white Farsi writing woven into it.

This rare group of carpets was highly prized. Oil had been discovered in the late nineteenth century under the lands of the Bakhtiyari in southern Persia. As the result of a deal with the Anglo-Persian Oil Company, the Bakhtiyari Khans became fabulously wealthy. One of the things they did with that wealth was to set up ateliers to produce finer carpets than had ever been made by their people. Rather than making carpets in bulk for wholesale trade, they made individual carpets by special order. The name of the Khan who ordered the carpet, along with a tribute to the esteemed recipient of the carpet, would appear in a cartouche at the top end. This masterpiece had been ordered by Morteza Khuli Khan in 1917 for a General he wished to honor.

Words will not convey the glowing colors in such a carpet. The wool was carefully chosen and spun tightly. Light glistened off the tips of the pile. The saturation of the colors was both intense and harmonious. The drawing of the design was precise and graceful, recalling the classical beauty of ancient Persian tile work. I was profoundly moved by this work of immense beauty and the joy with which Magdi presented it to me.

He knew I had to be in Paris soon, and he feted me with marinated lamb chops, grilled in his fireplace. Many other dishes accompanied it, spicy vegetables and kabobs and other eastern delights. It was two in the morning before I tumbled into bed.

Chapter Twenty-Three
Elysium

THE TRAIN FROM ZURICH to Paris took a bit over four hours. I indulged myself with a first class seat. This entitled me to linen coverings on my head rest, instant service, and decent food and wine. The ride was different from the slow and bumpy Northeast Corridor at home. This was smooth and quiet, rather like a mobile first class hotel. Even after a pot of their coffee, the atmosphere was so relaxing that I slipped off to sleep. About an hour before arrival in Paris, I awoke and ordered a half bottle of Pinot Noir and a charcuterie plate. I was awake and refreshed as we pulled into the *Gare de Lyon*.

I'll admit to a certain boyish anticipation of our meeting. I planned to be at our suite before Athena landed. The hotel was located half way between Napoleon's victory column in the *Place Vendome* and the Tuileries Gardens. It was a predictably grand affair with high ceilings, tall windows and beautiful woodwork. She had a copy of our reservation. Rather than meeting at the airport, I would wait for her with champagne and oysters. I did not have any confirmation that she was actually coming. I stifled vague fears that she had sold the tickets and was touring New England on a new motorcycle. Ridiculous, I suppose, but so little in life is certain.

It was not until early afternoon the next day that she arrived. I had left instructions with the desk to order the refreshments while she was registering.

"Welcome to our *pied-a-terre*," I said as she swept in before the bellman. I sent him off with a few francs.

"This is lovely, Deck, and what a neighborhood!"

"I think you'll like it. May I give you the tour?"

The Fall of Declan Curtis

"Do I need walking shoes?"

"No shoes at all, my dear. Kick them off! Get comfortable."

She tossed her coat and slipped out of her shoes. She hooked my arm as we toured. The main salon was large with a high ceiling and ornate moldings on the plaster. We examined the decorative balcony and admired the non-working fireplace. I showed her a beautiful bedroom with a canopied bed and a luxurious bath with elaborate antique fixtures.

"Can't we just sleep for a day before we do anything else?"

Before I could answer, the bell rang at our door. I opened it and a cart was wheeled in with two dozen oysters, and bottle of vintage Ruinart Rose champagne, and a vase with a dozen white roses.

"You don't do things by halves, do you?"

"Think of life in terms of Zeno's paradox. If one only goes by halves, he will never arrive."

"Very cute. Where is it that you want to arrive?'

"I'm working on that, Athena. It's not perfectly clear to me yet."

I poured two flutes and we toasted to "the journey."

"What's that door?"

I opened it. She walked into a mirror image of the first bedroom.

"Are we expecting company?"

"We've only spent one night together. I didn't think a gentleman should assume anything on that basis. *Et voila:* our suite!"

Athena looked at me with bright eyes and moved in for a clinch. It was a while before we got to the rest of the champagne and oysters. Fortunately, they were on ice. When we did get to them, we curled up on the divan wrapped in the hotel's fleecy robes. Slurping bivalves never seemed so sexy. Then we decided to test the three hundred thread count Egyptian sheets.

We awoke late that evening.

"Come on, let's not waste our time in paradise. Put on something casual and we'll go look at the night."

We walked into the vast, cobblestoned *Place Vendome* and admired Napoleon's erection for a while. I droned on a bit about his savants who plundered Egyptian civilization while doing important research.

"You'll see an obelisk they stole a few blocks from here in the morning."

We walked as far as the Opera House before we headed back. We slipped into a café for espresso and cognac on the way. The evening air was as soft as lust. We said little to each other when we climbed into bed.

"Leave a 'do not disturb' card. Let's just sleep as long as we want."

It was eleven before we had showered and dressed. That's when two baths come in handy. We were definitely feeling peckish by then.

"Let's walk in another direction. We can get omelets and head for the Arc de Triomphe."

"I feel like such a tourist."

"We are tourists. Nothing is so ridiculous as people from Oshkosh pretending they belong here. Every time I go to a city for the first time, I get right on the double-decker bus and take the tour. It's a great way to get your bearings. It may be a little embarrassing to be on display like that, but no one really cares. The trick to being a civilized tourist is to be a civilized person."

We had omelets on the *Rue de Rivoli*. They were excellent but not as good as mine. I was admiring the obelisk when Athena was diverted by a crepe vendor. She was inordinately delighted by one with apricot jam.

The Fall of Declan Curtis

"You have a sugar habit, don't you?"

She raised her eyebrows and nodded emphatically while her mouth was still full of crepe.

I realized I knew very little about this woman. She was a lawyer, a travel writer, and somewhat athletic. I knew she was fond of oysters, sweet things, champagne and me. Well, that's a good start. It was a sparkling day as we approached the *Arc*.

"It's huge," she said.

"Yes, it surprises people. It's fifty meters high."

I drew her to a traffic island in the *Champs* and gestured towards the grand *arc*.

"Can you imagine a huge Nazi flag hanging from it, and Hitler reviewing a parade of his Stormtroopers down this avenue? I think of the French people, already having sacrificed tens of thousands of lives to prevent this, standing in shock as the invaders strutted before them."

"Those are somber thoughts for such a beautiful day. You should be wooing your lover, not brooding on the past."

"The great cities of the world are never in a finished state. Along with the accumulated levels of architecture, there are the accumulated levels of human experience. Everyone plunders Faulkner for the quote about the past not even being past. The reason is that it's true. The Romans, Charlemagne, the Sun King, the Revolution, it's all here with us now."

"Yes, I feel it, too. My time in Greece as a young student permanently changed my perspective. We dug sites where civilizations were piled upon each other. After that, it's hard to accept that any contemporary regime is the apex of civilization, or that it is indispensable to human progress. Life simply continues."

We were working our way back towards the hotel. I steered her onto the grounds of a restaurant where the whimsical architecture reminded me of a wedding cake.

Café Lenotre's main room is a charming dome, like the inside of a *Faberge* egg. It features a champagne bar with which I was quite familiar from previous visits. It was still late afternoon with a gentle rosy light settling on the scene, so I asked to be seated in the glass conservatory off the main dining room.

"I don't know if I'm ready for dinner yet, Deck."

"Nor am I, my dear. We have only one mission here and that is real French truffles. You suggested that I woo my lover. Well here it is, champagne and chocolate truffles. This is the most fun you can have with your clothes on."

We were a bit giddy when we left. The combination of alcohol, sugar, and the splendid setting made everything dreamlike. I told her that we had dinner reservations for nine that evening, but I withheld the venue.

"Let's sleep for a few hours before we go out," Athena suggested.

"Just sleep?"

"You know."

That evening we walked along the Seine to our dinner at Jules Verne in the Eiffel Tower.

"I didn't know there was a fine restaurant in the tower," she said as we boarded the private elevator to the dining room.

"Well, it's a small place, but the food is exquisite and it has the best view in Paris."

We were seated at a window table, as I requested.

"Deck, this is too wonderful," Athena said as she took in the illuminated landscape below.

"Guy De Maupassant hated this tower. He frequented a restaurant in it so that he didn't have to look at it," and added with my best Gallic shrug, " '*à chacun son goût.*' "

We meandered through a six course tasting menu. Each course was tiny and superb.

The sommelier was helpful and friendly. I chose to let

The Fall of Declan Curtis

him guide us and I didn't regret it. The experience was not so much one of eating as it was a whirl of texture and flavor experiences. It was not eating for sustenance. It was a grand tour of the palate. We didn't spend a lot of time in conversation. We were both in a state of sensory overload and happy to simply enjoy it.

"That was the most memorable dining experience of my life. Being with you is changing my attitude towards food. It's also going to keep me busy in the gym or they'll be too much of me," Athena said as we descended in the private elevator.

"It's not the sort of dining one does often, but it can be a peak experience. Let's sleep a lot tonight. I'd like to take you to Versailles tomorrow, my lady! Behind all the formal landscape is an old stable that's been turned into a wine garden. We can sit under the arbor and I'll recite William Blake to you until they toss us out."

"Are we ever going back to the real world?"

"Not if I can help it."

We drifted down the promenade by the Seine. The tower periodically sparkled behind us.

We crossed the Pont Notre Dame, an ancient bridge originally built by the Celts before the Romans came. As we strolled across, I mentioned that in 1499, it had collapsed under the weight of sixty houses which were built upon it. A bit of trivia always enlivens a conversation.

We stood before the cathedral's façade and I wrapped my arms around her from behind. I could feel her pulse as my cheek rested on her neck. We said nothing for a long while. We simply let the nine-hundred-year-old architecture soothe us and make our place in the world clear to us. After all, The Last Judgment is carved above the central entrance. I had to gently tug her to break the spell. She looked up at me with an open smile. Her eyes swallowed me whole. I had an urge to tell her I loved her.

John Jeremiah

But I just leaned into her smile and kissed her for a long time. That was enough.

It was midnight when we passed into the lobby. Athena stopped at the service desk for messages. The bellman handed her an envelope. She began to tear it open as we stepped into the elevator.

"Are your services urgently required in New York?"

"Oh my god," she said as her knees buckled. Her face blanched and she leaned against the wall, "Bob Dexter is dead. He's been murdered."

Chapter Twenty-Four
Defense

AS YOU WELL KNOW, I didn't care a lick for Bob. But this was disturbing. Why the hell would the crooks decide to kill him? They couldn't know I had set them up. This had to be doped out before anyone else got hurt. We needed to get back home and find out what was going on. Athena was upset and a bit frightened. I got us plane tickets for Boston.

"I need you to come home with me to the Port. You can communicate with work by phone, but you'll be safer with us until we figure out what is going on."

"OK, I'm sure you're right. But there's something I have to tell you, Deck."

"Yes?"

"I think Bob was doing something illegal. No, I don't *think* so, he was. I just don't know exactly what was involved."

"All right, let's sit down and talk this over. Exactly what do you know?"

"Well, I'm pretty sure that wasn't the first time he met Sal. I could see the way they looked at each other the night of the exchange."

"What else?"

"There were two other similar 'buy-backs' since I started working there. I don't know what else may have happened before then. I've only been there a little over two years. But Bob seemed a little full of himself after those two deals. He spent a lot more money than his salary would justify."

"Well, that's not proof. Many men live beyond their means."

"It's more than that, more than the clothes and fancy

The Fall of Declan Curtis

restaurants. He was coming on pretty heavy to me. I wasn't interested, although I had dinner with him a few times."

"Can't blame him for liking you."

"He was persistent, and somewhat vulgar. He insinuated that he was doing very well 'outside the office.' He wanted to impress me. It didn't take a lot of insight to see that he was benefiting from these deals."

I got an uncomfortable feeling about this woman I thought I loved.

"Athena, you're an officer of the court. If you knew about a crime, you were bound to report it."

"I know, Deck, of course. And I knew that I could get him to talk if I played him along. But I'm not Bulldog Drummond. I was all alone and it was easier to ignore whatever he was up to."

I looked at her and understood her vulnerability. But I couldn't help wondering if there were more surprises. Did she know more than she was saying? I even had to question whether she was involved. I knew I had to make a decision about this, about her. Gus likes to say, "a man can't keep one foot on the boat and the other on the dock for very long." Was it right for me to judge her for not having the courage to bring down that crook by herself? Self-righteousness would be rich, coming from someone who had killed two men during that same year. I decided to go with believing in her, and not the least of my reasons was that the world would make no sense at all without her.

"Athena, is that all? Is there anything else he did or you did that you haven't told me?"

"No Deck, that's all. I have no evidence, just my suspicions."

"OK, you'll have to tell all of that to Red. And then you'll probably have to tell it all over again to a couple of investigators. That's just how it is. Don't hold anything back and don't change a word of your story."

"I understand. I'm the lawyer, remember? May I ask you about something I think you are holding back?"

"Sure, what's on your mind?"

"What made you get that tattoo?"

"I guess you have a right to an explanation. Here's the short version. I was married once. Her name was Anne. We were happy for about five years. Then there was a gradual estrangement. Finally, she disappeared with a friend of ours. He was a sailor and a charming seducer of discontented women. They were gone for about two months. In one episode, I had lost my wife and one of my closest friends. I found it hard to live with. I've always been a blues fan. But then I realized on a profound level what Robert Johnson meant. I had been mistreated, the world had paled. I wasn't suicidal, I was profoundly disillusioned. And I didn't mind dying."

"Pardon me for saying this, but there's quite a bit of self-pity in that."

"Sure," I laughed, "sure there is. That's a lot of what the blues are all about. But it doesn't make it any less real or painful."

~ ~ ~

Gus picked us up at the airport. It was about an hour to the Port. I explained about the late Mr. Dexter and the abortive deal with Sal and his crew.

"Deck, you shouldn't be allowed out alone."

"I'm in no position to argue that. But that's how it is. If Bob was in with them, it makes sense that they would want to eliminate him."

"No offense, Athena," Gus said over his shoulder, "but if you were involved with them, or even if they thought you knew his game, you could be next."

"She wasn't involved with them," I said with some irritation, "but you're right, she might be considered a loose end if they suspected that she was involved with Bob and knew his secrets."

"OK," Gus said, "Now we're getting practical. We'll be fine at the hotel. The third floor apartment is secure. I'll be on the second. We can put a few extra security men on around the clock for the duration. Unless they're willing to declare all-out war on you, you should be safe."

"You're right, Gus. And we'll know more after I talk to Red."

"Oh, and just in case you are interested," Gus said with theatrical sarcasm, "business has been good and your Swiss purchases are clearing customs now."

Athena was quiet as we rode the elevator to the third floor of the hotel. Once we were in my quarters she visibly relaxed. Her shoes were the first to go.

"I think I'll make a pot of Irish Breakfast tea. Do you want something stronger?"

"No, that sounds perfect, Deck."

So we settled down with tea and some chocolate wafers she clearly relished. I sat on an ottoman at her feet and massaged them. And we stayed for two weeks.

The next day I called Red and told him about Athena's information.

"We're a bit ahead of you there. It seems the company was already suspicious of Bob. They hadn't been able to define exactly what the scam was, but they knew it wasn't kosher. It would only have been a matter of time until he was caught. We'll take Athena's statement, but I don't think we need to make her come down here. Do you?"

Those last two words were fraught with meaning. We both knew what he was hinting at. He was asking me if I believed her.

"No, Red, I'm sure you don't need to waste your time dragging her down there. Let's get the bad guys."

"We often do, Deck. I'll keep you posted."

For the next two weeks we settled into the comfortable

John Jeremiah

routine of gallery owners. After breakfast on the third floor, we went down to my office by ten and answered correspondence.

Most clients came in by appointment, but there was a steady flow of walk-ins. The security guys were on the alert about unscheduled visitors. In my own kidding way, I introduced Athena to my friends and clients as "my attorney."

The Khan's Bakhtiyari carpet had cleared customs and been delivered to the gallery. Magdi had hand-washed it before showing it to me, so I was able to put it out on display without our usual cleaning in Denver. Athena and I had fun spreading it out in different directions until we had it just right. I called my German friend and client, Guenther, to come and see it. On a long walnut library table, I assembled reference material to help explain the piece. There were several hard cover books which touched on the subject. Most importantly, I displayed issues No. 43 and 44 of Hali magazine which contain an exhaustive article on this group. They are heavily illustrated with examples of the work, as well as photos of the many Khans who ordered these carpets and whose names appeared in them. I had some of Bach's sacred arias, which we both enjoyed, cued up on the sound system. I had two different single malts, a twenty-two-year old Ardbeg and a twenty-five year-old Springbank, at the ready.

"So, this is what it takes to charm your customers," Athena said.

"I know it seems that way, but it isn't so. I've learned you can't coax or cajole someone into buying a carpet. All things being equal, the carpet being first rate and a condition of trust existing between the actors, the decision is made within five or six seconds. It is made solely in the consciousness of the client. Sometimes they are not even fully cognizant of the event. But it is determined in

The Fall of Declan Curtis

moments. All the rest, the academics, the aesthetics, the music, the spirits, that's all just a cushion to enjoy while the decision is digested. I'm just the master of ceremonies while the event unfolds between the carpet and the client."

"You make it sound like you aren't necessary."

"Oh, not at all. This is where the "all things being equal" part comes in. I find, identify, and authenticate the art work. I guarantee it to be as represented. I do the research, provide the written documents, and address any condition issues like cleaning and restoration. I clear away all peripheral distractions and allow the event to proceed. Only at that point am I 'unnecessary'."

~ ~ ~

"Declan, *wie geht's, Dir denn?*" Guenther roared as he entered.

"Very well indeed, my friend. I'd like to introduce you to my attorney, Athena."

"A great pleasure, Madame," he purred from a slight bow as he kissed her hand.

The music was at a low volume but very atmospheric. I asked him to choose between the single malts, but his eyes were already fixed upon on the carpet.

"Look at the *hellblau* in this! Madame, have you ever seen such a blue?"

I chose the Springbank for him since I knew I had lost his attention. I served three strong fingers of it neat in a rocks glass.

"*Ach,*" he said as he let himself down into a comfortable arm chair, "*wohl bekomms!*"

"And to your health also, *mein Freund.*"

"There is something in this carpet which seizes the heart," he said, without raising his eyes.

"You see, Athena, my work is done."

We all had a good laugh. Guenther stayed for a dinner of oysters, shrimp, and arugula salad with a refreshing bottle of Chablis. We ate at the bar in the basement.

~ ~ ~

"This part of your business seems very pleasant, Deck," Athena said as she got into bed that night.

"That was a special transaction. Most business is more prosaic than that. But your point is well taken. It certainly beats having people pointing guns at you."

Athena tensed.

"Let's not go there," she murmured.

"No problem. I think we should go get some of your wardrobe. Or would you prefer we just went shopping?"

"I've got nothing against shopping, but I should get some of my own things, if you don't mind."

"We'll head down tomorrow."

Chapter Twenty-Five
"An Adequate of Hell"

GUS DROVE Athena and me to New York in the company van. We planned to get some of her belongings. She would continue to stay with me until things cleared up. From what Red told me, they thought that Dexter was even more deeply involved with the mob than Athena had suspected. They were going through his bank accounts and safe deposit boxes. Red couldn't give me any details. But without knowing everything Dexter and the mob were up to, it was impossible to know what they would do to cover it up. Red had a patrolman meet us at the apartment building.

"Officer, I'm Declan Curtis," I said to the only cop in the lobby.

"Good to meet you, sir. I'll take you upstairs. I suggest your friends stay here until we clear the premises."

"I like the way you think, Officer," I said as I peered at his tag, "O'Brian is it?"

Athena started to object, but I told her we wouldn't be long.

"Yes, please be patient," said O'Brien, "I'll be right back, folks."

The apartment was on the fifth floor. It was a solid pre-war building with a wide hallway. The parquet floor was buffed to a low sheen. A maroon Sarouk runner was buttoned down to the floor by brass snaps in the old-fashioned manner. Bronzed wall sconces with parchment shades cast a soft glow at regular intervals. A subtle "endless wave" motif was worked into the plaster where the wall met the gilded crown molding. Even the elevator door had a bold Art Deco V-shaped fold in the aluminum. I doubt the hall looked much different in 1935

The Fall of Declan Curtis

when The Courtland was built.

"They don't build 'em like this anymore," O'Brien said.

"Indeed they don't, Officer. And they're taking good care of this one. I've got the key here."

"Let me take that, sir. I'll just take a turn through to make sure it's secure."

"I never argue with an armed man," I said with a smile as I handed him the key.

He had a bit of a time with the lock. Finally, he got it to open just as he had a radio call.

As he turned to answer it, I slid past him into the foyer. It was dark in the apartment. All the shades were drawn. I felt my way to the living room and flipped the light switch. A loud crack was followed by a rolling ball of flame. I was blown off my feet. I was on fire. In the midst of intense pain, I could see myself rolling on the floor in an attempt to smother the flames. One part of me was screaming and struggling to put myself out. Another part of me was watching the scene at a remove and deciding what to do. I made it to my feet and ran right into O'Brien in the foyer. He grabbed me around the shoulders.

"Jesus, Jesus," I could hear him say as he helped me into the common hall. He shut the door on the burning apartment and radioed for help. I was vaguely aware of people running in the hall. But my consciousness was internal. My eyes were shut tight. All of my energy was concentrated on withstanding my pain. Skin was sloughing off my hands and the side of my face.

The sickening, acrid smell of burning hair made me retch. My clothing was still smoldering as I struggled to breathe. My heart was racing. I felt I was dying. And for the first time in a long time, I did mind.

"Stay with me, Curtis," said O'Brien, "this ain't gonna kill you. Just stay with me; help'll be here soon."

I was still awake when the EMTs arrived. They got me

onto a cart, attached an IV, and rolled me away. I was unconscious before the elevator doors closed

~ ~ ~

I came to in the operating room. They were cutting away all my clothing and assessing the extent of my wounds. I couldn't see out of my right eye. My whole body was quaking as if I were in a freezer. I was trying to keep my right hand elevated so it didn't come into contact with anything.

"You're going to be fine Deck," said a calm voice from a busy man. "You've got some bad burns but we're going to take good care of you. I've started you on something for the pain while we clean you up. You're in a little shock but that should get better soon. Can you breathe OK?"

I managed to squeak out a "Yeah."

~ ~ ~

The first time I woke up in my hospital room, Gus was there.

"I knew I shouldn't have let you go up there alone, you dumb bastard."

"Why Gus, that's the nicest thing you've ever said to me."

"Fuck you. You gonna be all right?"

"Pretty much, I think. I'm worried about my eye."

"Don't worry about it. I talked to your doctor. He says your vision will clear up when the swelling goes down. Your right hand is going to need some rehab and maybe some grafting."

"So why are you asking me if I'm all right? You obviously know more about it than I do."

"There's another thing, too. I hate to break it to you, but you're not going to be as pretty as you were."

"Damn, boy, women like a man with a few scars and an eye patch. Maybe I'll get a parrot, too. Speaking of women, have you seen Athena?"

The Fall of Declan Curtis

"She's been here all along, but she's taking it pretty hard. I'll let her know you're able to talk."

"I think I'm done for now." As much as I wanted to see her, I was feeling tired and the pain had overtaken the morphine. "Tell her tomorrow, OK?"

"Sure, just one more thing. Uncle called the Gallery. I gave him an update on your condition. He said to tell you he would do anything you needed."

"From most people, that's easy to say. But when Uncle says 'anything' that encompasses a lot. Send him a note that 'rumors of my demise are greatly exaggerated.' Tell him I think everything is under control. I'll call him from home when I get out. And tell him I said thanks."

~ ~ ~

When Athena finally saw me, both my hands were in splints and wrapped in gauze. My eye was starting to open, but my face was bright red and ragged on the right side. They had shaved my head, and my eyebrows had been burned off. She had to wear a surgical mask to prevent infection. She couldn't speak. They kept the room at about a hundred degrees for burn patients. I hoped she wouldn't pass out.

"Hey, kiddo, you look mysterious in a mask. Is this a kinky sex thing or are you here to rob me?"

I couldn't tell if she laughed or choked. Her eyes welled up.

"I'm so sorry, Deck. I... I don't know what to say."

"You've got nothing to be sorry for. We are Belle et la Bête, it seems. I am a beast now but I'll be beautiful again if you'll just kiss me."

"Don't touch anything," I said as she reached for me, "I'll get around to that later, if you'll still have me."

"Even now, you can't be serious."

"Oh Belle, I'm serious all right. I'm already planning meals for when I get out of here. The River Café will be our first date. Our own beautiful Cleopatra's barge under the Brooklyn Bridge."

"Be serious. What are we going to do? They may try this again."

"Listen to me carefully. Don't give that another thought. Gus and I will take care of that."

"But you have no idea who we are up against."

"I'll give you three to one odds that the cops already know exactly who they are after."

"But these are clearly dangerous thugs."

"Athena, the truth is, they'll probably be apprehended before I even get well enough to do anything. Red and his boys are all over this, and the FBI too. Remember, they might have killed O'Brien. The force frowns on that. By the way, I need to talk to Red. I don't want O'Brien to get in trouble for not being the first one in. Tell Gus, will you?"

"Sure, Deck, I hope you are right."

Of course, I wasn't being completely frank with her. I yearned for some revenge on the animals who did this to us. But there seemed little point in having Athena worry about that now. I didn't even know myself what I planned to do, or how long it would take me to be fit enough to do it. But I was savoring the idea.

"I'm about worn out now, but I want you to know something important. We've only had a short time together. I don't have to tell you what it's meant to me. I know you're swamped with a host of emotions now. The next few months are not going to be easy or fun. Look at me," I said to focus her attention. "If it's time for you to move on and take care of yourself, it's OK. 'No hard feelings', remember? I'll understand."

"Why are men so stupid?"

I gave her my best idiot grin.

" 'We'll always have Paris.' " I said.

Chapter Twenty-Six
Sharks

I HEARD THE SHARKS before I saw them. Rhythmic swishing sounds announced them as they turned each corner of the bed. My hands were still in splints, and half of my face was covered in gauze. I managed to tip myself up on an elbow and peer over the side of the bed. I had to turn my head awkwardly to get a line of sight for my good eye. The water was an unhealthy green. The first shark threw up some foam as he came around. I was wet all over, but I didn't think I'd been in the water. I wasn't afraid. I simply wouldn't go in. I lay back down into the soggy sheets. I saw everything through a haze. It was hard to bring anything into sharp focus. And it felt as if the bones in my hands were on fire.

"Deck, Deck, can you hear me?"

At first I thought it was my dead father. But he was in doctor's scrubs.

"Watch out for the sharks!" I said, as I waved my splints.

"Take it easy, Deck, I have them under control. Nothing for you to worry about. Can you understand me?"

"Sure."

"Listen, you're going to be fine. But we have a problem. You've got an infection. It is causing a very high fever. We'll have it under control soon."

"I got something else?"

"Yes, sort of. Try not to worry about things that seem strange, like sharks. It's all part of your fever. It's a hundred and five now. When it comes down, everything will seem much better. Believe me," he said in a calm cadence.

"I'll be better? Like I'll be lying in a hospital bed all

The Fall of Declan Curtis

burned up but no fever? That's something to look forward to." It came out more angry than I'd intended.

"Well, I'm glad you can indulge in some sardonic humor. I guess that shows you're improving already. But being conscious and in pain beats being frightened and delirious. It's all relative. And you'll improve after that, as well. Once we have the infection beat, you'll be out of here shortly."

The more he talked, the more I was able to focus on something external. It didn't make the pain go away, but it distracted me enough to make it move a bit into the background. I could hear his footsteps on the tile floor. That broke the illusion of floating on water.

"I'm going to have some of the girls come in and change these sheets and sponge you off. Then we'll get you your afternoon shot and perhaps you can get some sleep."

Two student nurses helped me off the bed and onto a chair. Not for the first time, I felt like Frankenstein's monster. They carefully slid my damp "jonnie" over my splinted hands. They had me stand naked for a few minutes with my forearms resting on the chair-back while they sponged me off. In an attempt to feign poise, I regaled them with the story of FDR walking into the guest bedroom at the White House during the War. He surprised a naked Churchill who had just stepped out of his bath. "As you can see Mr. President, England has nothing to hide," he quipped. The girls giggled, but I was unsure whether they knew who either of those men were. They sat me back down with a clean "jonnie" while they changed the sheets. My bare ass, with no coverage from the hospital "jonnie", stuck to the vinyl seat and made a sort of Velcro noise as they lifted me off the chair. This elicited a bigger giggle than my historical yarn. So often in life, a bit of slapstick trumps the wittiest anecdote.

Even when your balance is not compromised by fever

and exhaustion, maneuvering yourself with no hands is a challenge. Try getting up on a high bed without using your mitts. The kids had to do a bit of engineering to get me back up onto the newly made bed without any help from me. Once in, I could adjust my position from my elbows. The cotton seemed cool, and so did the morphine drip. For a short while, I relaxed.

Then a masked crew burst into the room and held me down. The leader waited for them to rip the bandages from my hands. Then he started to cut and scrape my wounds. I screamed a bit and called them foul names. It seemed like they tormented me for hours but I refused to tell them what they wanted to know.

"That's all for now. The other hand looks fine. We'll look at the face in the morning."

When the Nazi bastards left, the pain in my right hand was unbearable. I felt they had burned it all over again. It throbbed as if the pain and blood would burst through my skin in an explosion. In my delirium I couldn't remember what information they wanted, but I took some pride in knowing I had not given them anything.

~ ~ ~

My temperature was back to normal a few days later. The doctor explained "debridement."

"You had a bad time of it, Deck. I know it was terrifying for you to go through that in your confused mental state. It's outright torture in the best of circumstances. It's something we don't look forward to performing either. But the dead tissue has to be removed surgically from burned areas so the healthy tissue can heal."

"Unfortunately, Doc, I recently read *The Rise and Fall of the Third Reich*. Somehow that colored my hallucinatory world. I thought you were torturing me for information."

"Yes, I remember you calling us Nazis and other unpleasant things," he said with a careful grin. I think he

The Fall of Declan Curtis

was testing my ability to appreciate the sad humor in the circumstance.

"Sorry Doc, but even if I weren't out of my mind with a fever, I'd still call you names if you held me down and peeled my skin off."

"Fair enough, Deck. The good news is, that's all over and the small graft we took from your thigh has done quite well on your hand. We're going to keep an eye on your wounds for a few days. Then, if it all still looks good, we'll send you home."

"Please make it as soon as you can. By the way, what kind of Scotch do you like?"

"I've heard from Gus that you are a connoisseur. My taste is fairly mundane. Why don't you surprise me?"

"Deal."

"If I may make a personal observation, you've sure got a lot of fight in you for someone who 'don't mind dyin'.'"

"*Touché*, Doc. But even a man who hangs himself kicks at the end."

"Well, that's a vivid metaphor."

"Like suicide, tattoos can be a permanent response to a temporary feeling. I was at a very low point in my life when I did that."

"It takes time to gain perspective," Doc said.

"Indeed it does, but I wasn't entirely wrong. I've seen enough of life to know that our reasons to live may be snatched away at any time. Life alone is no reason to live."

"But Deck, while you have life you have possibilities."

"Possibilities, yes, for good and for unimaginable sorrow. We're all tied to the wheel of life. When you're at the bottom it crushes you. I'm on the rise now, but the wheel is always turning."

"That's rather fatalistic."

"Jeremiah Murphy once wrote in the *Boston Globe* that to be Irish means to know that this life will eventually break your heart."

"I see you're determined to savor the dark side. I'll leave you with your cheery thoughts now. You've got some visitors waiting."

"Thanks for everything, Doc."

I was seeing with both eyes now. No more bandages on my head or my left hand. My face was a vigorous shade of red but healing well. I would have some pretty good scars from my right cheek back to my ear which would look like a boxer's cauliflower. All in all, I was pretty lucky, and I knew it. Gus and Athena came in.

"They're planning to spring you on Wednesday if you don't go nuts again."

"I'll do my best, Gus. Grand to see you Belle. As my sainted grandfather told me on his deathbed, 'seeing you is like finding a thousand-dollar bill.'"

"Well, that has a certain kind of poetry to it, but you're not on a deathbed. I've been here in New York dealing with things all week, and I'll be back here to take you home on Wednesday," she said.

"You think it's wise to be down here alone?"

"That's the big news we have for you," Gus said with enthusiasm. "Remember your pal, Sal, who ran the heist?"

"Sure I do. I'm hoping to dance with him again someday."

"Well, you missed your chance. His card is full. Red told us they found him in Brooklyn. One in the chest and one in each eye. The cops figure his boss gave him a chance to get rid of the only two people who knew him. So it was Sal who shot Bob. But when he blew the hit on Athena, whoever runs the show decided to cut off his connection to the crimes. With Sal gone, no one can trace the conspiracy any further. The two drivers are co-operating, but they never had contact with anyone higher up than Sal either. So they can't help the cops any further. That should leave you two in the

The Fall of Declan Curtis

clear. Since you never met anyone else in the scheme, you can't hurt them. It all stops with Sal."

"That's all good. But someone ran that racket and it looks like he'll get away with it."

"Well Deck, you're just going to have to be satisfied that the thug who went after you guys is dead. You're not the FBI. You can't take down a mob by yourself. Be satisfied with winning your battle. Leave the war to the pros."

I began to brood.

~ ~ ~

"Deck," said Athena, "I've been talking to Anne outside. She just wants to see you."

I didn't reply for a long time.

"I think you should, Deck," Athena coaxed, "put it behind you."

"Sure, OK."

Anne looked good. She had lost some weight, not that she needed to. But all women seem to lose weight when they become single. I guess they instinctively freshen up the bait for the next go-around. She was on edge and tentative. I could see horror in her eyes as she looked over my wounds.

"I know, it looks bad. But I'll be quite myself in a month or two. No permanent damage."

"I don't know what to say, Deck. I'm so sorry this has happened to you."

"It's all right, Anne, really. Things are going well for me in the big picture. It's very kind of you to come and see me. I hope you're happy now. I apologize for the unpleasant scene at the loft. I've had a few years to think things over. You had your reasons for doing what you did. My preoccupation with myself was just one of them. "

All of this was true. None of it justified running off with Gator instead of addressing our issues or at least breaking up with me before leaving. But none of that mattered now. I just wanted to finish this conversation in a civilized manner and be done with it.

"Thanks, Deck. I've met Athena. She's beautiful and smart. I like her. Is it serious?"

"Well, I like her a lot. It's only been a few months. We'll see. How about you?"

"I'm not seeing anyone seriously, still just getting my balance."

"I hope you find happiness and I hope you forgive me for my mistakes."

"Of course, Deck, I'm glad we had this conversation."

"Me, too."

Chapter Twenty-Seven
A Crazy Idea

AFTER A MONTH at home in the hotel, I was moving my hands pretty well. The physical therapist had me flexing a spring loaded mechanism. The blue-handled contraption was becoming part of my image. It was always with me and frequently in motion. I discovered that muscles degrade very quickly when they are immobile. My right hand was so weak after it's time in splints that I couldn't effectively write my name. But using the flexor built up hand strength almost as quickly as it had been undone. The other important therapeutic effect was stretching the skin on my hands as they healed, especially the right one. Skin tends to tighten up as it heals from burns. If it is not stretched constantly, it will shrink and result in a loss of movement. So I worked it hard. My face didn't hurt much anymore, except for my ear itself. That was tender and I tried not to sleep on that side. It looked rather raw but I was fine. I had long since given up the codeine pills and my eyesight was normal again.

Athena commuted regularly to New York but spent at least a third of her time up in the Port. I knew she liked being here, but she adamantly clung to her work. Well, that's not precise. It was her identity as a lawyer, her independence that she was clinging to. She had worked hard to get where she was. Her satisfaction with operating in the world, wielding power, and earning respect was as strong as any man's. I was careful to keep plenty of breathing room in our lives. Neither of us would tolerate crowding.

"What's on the schedule?" Athena asked.

"Well, Atwater will be here this afternoon for a

The Fall of Declan Curtis

photography session. I'm assembling our first hard-cover catalogue for the fall. I'm enjoying the work but it takes up a lot of time. And I've been working on the text as well."

"Is there anything I can do to help?"

"Well, you can help us with the shoot if you like. You might find the process interesting. If you get bored, you can always slip off. Or you can edit my deathless prose, if you like that sort of thing. If none of that interests you, we can just play hooky at the basement bar and drink champagne."

"All of the above sound like fun. But we'll enjoy the bubbles more after we've earned them with some work."

The photography was a tedious process. Multiple lights had to be positioned and light meters used to confirm proper illumination. Then we took big black and white Polaroids which revealed our degree of success with lighting. Once that was settled, we shot 4" x 5" transparencies at several settings for each rug. Then we carefully packaged them in the dark and sent them off to a lab. If there were good ones when they came back, they were then sent to color separators who made films in four colors for printing. At every stage, things could go wrong. The worst trouble was with the printers. They just couldn't grasp the color values that we were reaching for. Fortunately, my patience was boundless.

We managed about four hours of work before we decided to quit and retire to the bar.

"I've had another conversation with Red while you were away," I said as I uncorked the wine.

"Anything new?"

"Yes and no. It seems the company has discovered a pattern while cooperating with the FBI. They now suspect that Bob not only took kickbacks from the exchanges, but that he may have been a part of a wider scheme in the industry to identify prime targets for the thieves."

"He set up our customers to be robbed?"

"It seems to be a probability. They've detected a pattern among three insurance companies. They were too greedy. Instead of spreading out the crimes, they went for clusters of highly insured clients. It just left too many obvious connections. Perhaps they felt that since most of the stolen goods were being returned, no one would analyze what was going on and see the pattern."

"There were other adjusters doing what Bob did?"

"Evidently. The FBI has identified two others they think were involved. Each worked for a different insurer. No one knows if any of the three knew each other."

"Were they working for the same gang as Bob?" Athena asked.

"Who knows? Unless the FBI is successful and we read about it in the newspapers, I doubt we'll get any more inside information. Frankly, I'm a little surprised Red told me this much. I guess he thought we deserved a little explanation about what happened to us."

"Well, at least we're out of it."

"Yes, indeed." I said, even as a crazy idea began to haunt me.

At the end of the week I drove Athena back to Manhattan. She had found a smallish one bedroom in a pre-war building on Park Avenue South. Most of her belongings were lost in the fire, so she had little baggage. Her utilitarian *pied-a-terre* didn't compare to the elegant apartment she'd had at The Courtland. Of course, she could have moved back there when its renovation was complete. But the memory was not a pleasant one for her. Anyway, a small place made sense, since she was living with me much of the time. I didn't voice this thought to her, but I took her choice as an indicator of how seriously she viewed our unfolding relationship.

There was a cute but painfully narrow little balcony. When she was alone, she liked to have a quiet breakfast,

The Fall of Declan Curtis

squeezed in there with some yogurt and other healthy things. The part I liked, when I was there, was walking to Les Halles for an indulgent breakfast. And the Oyster Bar in Grand Central was even closer. It was perfect.

"Have a good day. I have a few meetings, both at uptown galleries and downtown in the wholesale district. I'm going to try to get out of town by three. But if I'm here much later than that, I'll be looking for lodging."

"I think I have a vacancy if you'll spring for dinner."

"That's the best offer I've had all day. I'll call."

"*Ciao, ciao.*"

I really did have a few appointments for rug business. But I blew them off. I was up to mischief. It was not a fully formed idea, and certainly no sort of plan. But I had a primordial urge to which I had to bend.

The precinct steps were foot-worn slabs rising to a ponderous Greek Revival granite building which would have benefitted from a nice steam cleaning. It could have been almost beautiful. The bronze lanterns flanking the entrance were substantial and nicely patinated. A long row of squad cars were parked at an angle to the curb, and not too carefully. I walked in and announced to the desk Sergeant that I was here to see Red.

"Well, you're looking much improved, Deck," Red said while taking a visual inventory.

"Things are pretty much back to normal," I said as I sat on an ancient oak armchair.

"You still keeping company with that beautiful lawyer?"

"For as long as she'll have me."

"If you'll take a bit of advice from an old man, don't let her get away boyo."

"Well, if she takes off, I'll file the missing persons with you, Red."

"OK, enough Blarney. What are you here for?"

"I really appreciate the info on the investigation. I'm

curious, do you think the other adjusters were working for the same gang?"

"Hold on there, Deck, we can't prove any conspiracy yet. If we don't know what they did, we certainly don't know who they worked for."

"Look Red, I understand procedure. Of course we can't sling unproven charges around publicly. I'm just asking you, privately, what is your surmise?"

"My own suspicion is that this was run by one mob," Red began with an air of resignation, "they got to at least three men who we think we have identified. One was your friend Bob Dexter. As you know, they got rid of him."

"Shouldn't that scare the hell out of the other two?"

"There you go again, Deck, skipping right to the end of the story. Do you read books that way?"

"OK, OK. I know I'm too anxious, but I've got some skin in this game."

"I understand. Have you considered that the FBI may not have confronted their suspects yet? They're very conservative and methodical. They won't alert the suspects until they can present them with overwhelming proof. Of course, once they do, the danger they are in will be explained to them in gory detail. I imagine that'll be ample motivation to get the suspects to cooperate. We'll just have to wait and see how it unfolds. The FBI doesn't report to me. And, I might point out, I don't report to you."

I realized I'd gone too far.

"Red, I know I'm being a pain in the ass. I'm sorry. I'll leave you alone about this."

"No harm, boyo. Have you had lunch?"

"No, and I'm starving. Can I take you to Eamonn Doran's for steak and kidney pie?"

"That sounds like a bribe to me, and I'll be takin' it."

After an enjoyable lunch, I skipped rug business for the day. Instead, I headed to the Public Library on Fifth

Avenue. This gargantuan pile of stone, like the Met, is a tribute to classical Greece and Rome. I passed the lions that guarded it and entered the magnificent hall. Fluted walnut columns reached up towards the vaulted ceiling. As they did when I was here as a boy with my dad, Moses cast his tablets down upon the rocks while Prometheus flew overhead with his stolen fire. I pulled myself away and got to work researching the biggest insurance companies servicing the upper tier of New York society. There were more than a few, naturally. Then I cross-referenced those with newspaper accounts of high profile burglaries in town over the last two years.

I found a few small notices of "recoveries" as well, but they had scant details. I'm sure the companies didn't want their embarrassing business sorted out in public. The only exception among recovery stories was the sensational coverage of the material I had vetted. It was big news for the hero cops who brought in the big haul. And it was easy fun for the journalists who ridiculed the dumb thieves who got caught over a "broken tail light." I casually wondered how many other things I had read in the papers with confidence were as spurious as this story. They also diverted themselves with Bob's tale of being arrested with the thieves and having to convince the cops he was a hostage. I turned up a small notice about Bob being found dead, but no connection was made with his work or his part in the robbery.

The insurance companies could limit the stories about recoveries but they couldn't prevent the reporting of big burglaries. I narrowed the candidates to five companies that had an unusual number of incidents. And among them, the bulk of crimes were committed against three companies. Without "jumping to the end of the story," I thought I may have found our list. I didn't know quite where to take it from there, but I thought I had a good start. How to find out who might be involved? I had an idea about that, too. I put in a call to my college pal, Bill Scheller, at the *New York Times*. I left a message that he should try to clear some time for me but it would have to wait until tomorrow.

Then I called Athena from the library and had her meet me at the *Café Des Artistes* for dinner. All this information was percolating in my mind, but I'd keep it to myself and enjoy some down time with my goddess of wisdom. It was almost past twilight when I got there. The building was granite with Tudor details and wide Gothic arches over the windows. A soft yellow light emanated through the leaded glass panes. Stepping inside was like entering a *Mittel-European* café in the early twentieth century. Naked ladies frolicked in large paintings. The impression was odd though. While nymphs posing in Edenic woodlands was a classical convention, these nymphs were curiously modern and seemed more naked and *risqué* for all that. Athena and I liked this quirky place for many reasons. For instance, they served Heidsieck Monopole by the glass. When one didn't want to tackle a whole bottle and at the same time didn't want to settle for something second rate, this was convenient.

"You're having the duck confit, aren't you?" Athena asked.

"Won't you at least let me peruse the menu and pretend I am considering something else?"

"And who do you think you'll be fooling?"

I smirked at her. How could we have reached this level of intimacy in just six months?

"So, how did your day go?"

"I had lunch with Red and I did some research at the Public Library. It was a productive day."

"Did he tell you anything new?"

"In a way, he did. He told me to stop bothering him. He reminded me that 'he doesn't report' to me."

The Fall of Declan Curtis

"Ouch, that sounds awkward."

"It was for a moment but we decided to let it go. I took him to lunch at Eamonn Doran's on Second Avenue."

"I don't know that one."

"It's an Irish joint that makes a great steak and kidney pie. They make it with a real suet crust. Perfect lunch with a pint or two of Guinness."

"Do you ever even consider a salad for lunch?"

"Only in so much as I consider becoming a hairdresser."

Chapter Twenty-Eight
Old Pals

BILL INVITED ME to lunch at a saloon near the *Times* building where reporters hung out. I told him I'd rather meet where no one would know or care what we were talking about. On a whim I suggested McSorley's Old Ale House in the village. We had wasted many a collegiate hour there having earnest discussions about life, death, war, and other things we knew little or nothing about. In those days, women weren't even allowed in the bar; they were just another subject we were ignorant about. I told him to bring his notebook.

"OK, Deck, what's the big mystery?" Bill said as he wrapped me in a bear hug.

"It's going to be a long story. Let's get some refreshments."

After we had lined up several mugs of ale, I started to fill him in on the story. I handed him a folder containing my research from the library. He took plenty of time to read the print outs. I also included a written a summary of the events and my theories. He had the papers spread out across the beer-stained table. When he eventually seemed to relax and began to drink his ale, I spoke up.

"Look Bill, you have to keep this to yourself until we know what's going to happen. This could be a big story for you. But I don't want to piss off the cops or the FBI by messing up their investigation. We have to be careful."

"Let's be clear, Deck. You say there has been a conspiracy conducted by a criminal enterprise to burglarize very wealthy homes. They suborned insurance company employees to identify potential victims. Then they sold the goods back to the insurer. And you have no idea who they

The Fall of Declan Curtis

might be. Am I right so far?"

"Yes. I stumbled into the operation at the lowest level. They murdered one of the men I had met. Then they tried to murder my attorney and blew me up instead. I have no leads left. I only have the circumstantial evidence I just gave you."

"Well, I've investigated stories with less evidence than this, though not always to a successful conclusion. I can certainly see the pattern here. I'll have to get my editor's OK to block out some time for this, but that won't be a problem. We'll have our researchers do what you started yesterday but with more extensive resources. We'll find out who the adjusters are for your list of companies. We can look into their lives for signs of big spending or other lifestyle changes. You're right, it will make a great feature if it breaks as a big conspiracy. The murder will be the icing. But let me ask you something. What's in it for you? It seems you're off their radar now. Why ask for more trouble?"

"They set me on fire, Bill. And I love the woman they tried to kill. I want them to go down for this. There's a good chance that the authorities will settle for the adjusters if they feel they can't go higher up. I won't. I want the bosses and I want to know I was part of their undoing."

"OK, Eliot Ness, I get it. It's personal for you. Once we've done our research, we can start to do some low-key interviews. We'll go to the insurers and say we're doing a little crime story about burglaries in Manhattan. We can present it so that they'll see the story as positive PR, showing how well they take care of their clients after a loss. Then we can interview their adjusters without alerting them."

"That sounds great, Bill. There's nothing more I can do on my own without raising alarms. But you can move in on them under the cover of your job."

"I'm sure we'll figure out who the crooked adjusters are.

That's the easy part. But at that point, we'll have to make some decisions. Do we simply turn them in to the FBI? The truth is, the Feds might catch them before we even know who they are. And anyway, if we do identify them first, what can we do on our own to make them talk? The paper frowns on kidnapping and torture."

"I'm not suggesting we become vigilantes, Bill," I managed to say that without irony, despite my recent history, "but even if they beat you to the punch, you'll have a great story ready to print before your competition can even see the big picture."

"I don't need any selling. This is good. I'll keep you close to the investigation, but you have to let me do it my way. OK?"

"You keep me dialed in and I'll keep my thoughts to myself, Bill. Ready for another?"

"Always ready."

Neither of us felt like going over the story again that night. We nursed our thoughts and our ale.

"They've still got the bones up there," I said.

Bill looked at the ancient gas fixture above us with its furry grey wishbones hooked over the cross bar. We had done some rather vigorous protesting of the Vietnam War in the '60s. Now that we were mature men, those bones were more profoundly stirring. Young soldiers embarking from New York to the Great War ate chicken dinners here. The doughboys hung up the wish bones for good luck, hoping to return and take one down. Some seventy years later, many of them were still up there.

"I'm ready to eat. Maybe I'll call Chris and have him meet us?"

Chris was a photographer for the *Times* and an old pal of Bill's. He was a classic hard drinking, chain smoking newspaperman. His idea of heaven was a bottle of Jack Daniels on the bar and the Rolling Stones on the speakers,

The Fall of Declan Curtis

loud. And every five years or so, he either got married or divorced. The three of us were slightly dangerous together.

"Sure, Bill. Let's have him meet us at the Minetta."

Bill and I were on our second whiskey when Chris burst in. We had already decided to bring him into the whole story. I could still smell the unfiltered Camel that he had just thrown down outside the entrance.

"Hey, what are you two up to?"

He had a funny, crooked sort of grin. He pushed up his black-rimmed glasses and watched us with zany anticipation. We gave him a brief rundown and ordered him some Jack. Bill and I played with some oysters while Chris looked over the clippings and summaries.

"Good story if we can get inside. You going for it, Bill?"

"Yeah, full tilt, Chris."

"What about you, Deck. You tryin' to get killed next time?"

Chris was not subtle. He reminded me of Gus that way.

"Well, Chris, I might get killed next time around but I'm sure I can depend on you to get the photo."

"Yes you can, even if I have to re-arrange your limbs for aesthetic reasons."

The world came up a few steaks short and with several fewer bottles of Montepulciano by the end of that evening.

Chapter Twenty-Nine
Our First Argument

ATHENA AND I had been back in the Port for three weeks since my dinner with Bill. The material for the catalogue had been sent off to the printers in Ohio. I'd be getting proofs back in a few more weeks. It was a relief to have that work behind me. We were planning an exhibition with the catalogue in the fall. The staff at the gallery had learned to function well without my daily presence. Having me "in-house" for three consecutive weeks was an adjustment. I shared a lot of the business plan with my general manager, Peter. He was more than competent to run with it while I was away, either working or recovering in hospitals.

I'd been sharing the details of the business with Athena as well. She seemed to be interested in both the retail end and the practical business of finance and tax structuring. We had heard from Uncle that week. He wanted to have a meeting soon. He announced that he would be in New York at the Plaza next month and would I have dinner with him? This was a rhetorical question, of course. I would meet him anytime. I replied politely that I would be delighted and if he would forward his dates to me, I would also reserve a suite there for myself and my attorney. Then Bill called.

"Hey, Deck. I think we've got our boys lined up. One of them is with Highland Assurance. He's a chief adjuster by the name of Fred Hawling. He's thirty-two with a wife and two kids. He makes forty-five thousand a year and lived in a hundred-and-thirty- thousand dollar house in a development on Long Island until recently."

"Until recently?"

"Yes, it seems Freddy has been saving his pennies. He just bought a three-hundred-and-fifty-thousand dollar place further out on the island."

"How nice for him."

"Our other suspect is a James Coffee who works as an adjuster for Lincoln Group Insurance. He's not the top guy. He's making thirty-five thousand. He's single and he's not doing any big spending."

"So, why do you think he's the one?"

"Well, he's living below his earning level. He's in a rented room rather than a home. It's not much better than a flophouse. He looks a bit seedy, not bad enough to draw attention at work, but his wardrobe is pretty tired looking."

"Booze or drugs?"

"Neither, it looks like Jimmy's got a gambling jones. One of the guys at the paper does a little betting with a bookie from Hell's Kitchen. He managed to find out from him that Jim's bookie is Harry the Hat. Without boring you with details, we found out from the Hat that our boy Jim has improved Harry's bottom line significantly this past year."

"How much improvement?"

"We don't have a financial sheet, but he hinted it was over a hundred large. We had to be subtle. Harry doesn't want to lose a sucker of that magnitude. Our guy simply suggested to the Hat that trouble might be following Jimmy, so Harry should be discreet. The Hat appreciated the tip."

"OK, what's next?" I asked.

"I think it's time to introduce our feature story writer, me, to the management at both Highland and Lincoln. Let's ask for some interviews and get the story rolling."

"Can I sit in when you get to the adjusters?"

"Definitely not, too unprofessional. If your cover was blown, I'd lose my job. Don't worry, I'll find out what you need to know. Then you can go see them on your own if you like, or just turn them over to your Detective pal. But you need to keep me in on what they are going to do so I'll know when to break my story. And an interview with Red would be most appreciated."

"I'm happy to try but I can't guarantee anything."

~ ~ ~

I didn't want Athena to be worrying about our safety but I couldn't, in good conscience, keep her out of the loop any longer. I invited her to sit with me in the office.

"There have been some developments I think you should know about. I've told Bill all about the insurance scheme."

"Why?"

"He's a newspaper guy and this is a great story. I'd like to find out who was behind it all, but I can't just invite people to tell me everything. As a reporter, he can."

"Aren't you worried about drawing attention to yourself, to us?"

"No, I don't see it that way. We're still out of contact with anyone involved. We can't hurt whoever is at the top of this. Bill can ask questions without tipping his hand about his real target."

"What if they figure out what he's up to?"

"Well, there is a certain amount of protection from his position. Traditionally, gangsters don't want the heat that comes from killing a reporter or a cop. Sure, it happens, but it's unlikely."

"I don't like this, Deck. It's irresponsible. Your duty as a citizen only goes as far as telling the police what you know. You're not a detective. I'm asking you to stay out of it."

"I'm not entirely clear about my duty as a citizen. But I know what my duty is as a man. They tried to kill you. They set me on fire. I won't even list the others they have corrupted or killed, that part isn't my business. But defending me and mine is my business. I'm just going to have to ask you to trust me on this. I have to do it."

The Fall of Declan Curtis

"And if you are killed?"

"There are men who will devote themselves to bring hell down upon the killers."

I couldn't believe I was saying this. I had laughed at Uncle and Red for suggesting the same thing. But there it was.

"And what about me?"

"Having a live man with no self-respect isn't a formula for happiness, Athena. I'll play this out as carefully as I can. And I'll turn it over to the FBI as soon as I can. But I have to do it. If you can't live with it, I'll be very sorry, but I'll understand."

"Sometimes I feel like I don't really know who you are, Deck."

I remembered hearing those same words years ago from Anne. In those days I let too much happen around me without responding. My internal life led to external passivity. Not anymore.

"This is me, Belle, this is who I am."

Chapter Thirty
Room 213

BILL'S CALL woke me up at Athena's apartment. He always got up around five a.m., but he knew better than to call me before nine.

"What?"

"Sorry Deck, wake the fuck up, this is important."

That did the trick.

"All right, let's have it."

"Freddie's dead."

"If you're playing 60s trivia, I'll kick your ass."

"No joke, Deck. Fred Hawling was murdered last night. We interviewed him three days ago."

"Shit. You think they're shutting the doors?"

"Hell yes."

"Did you get anything out of him?"

"Yeah, we got his confession and Chris took some pics, but no info to take us further up. Evidently, Sal was his only contact, too. He didn't know anyone else."

"You have to admit, they did a great job of insulating themselves from potential witnesses," I said to Bill.

"Evidently. We explained to him that the cops knew all about him. The only way to safety, the only way to help his case, was to go in and make a deal. Hawling promised to turn himself in to the FBI."

"And?"

"And he said that was what he was going to do."

"Clearly, he didn't do it fast enough. Bad timing. What about James Coffee?"

"I've had Chris waiting in Jim's rented room since we heard about Fred. Nothing, yet."

"OK, I think we'd better get over there. This isn't a

The Fall of Declan Curtis

newspaper interview any more. It's is an extraction, that is if he reaches us."

Athena was alarmed. My half of the conversation was revealing enough.

"Another one of the adjusters has been murdered. We're going to try to save the last one."

"Deck, come on, just call the cops. Don't get in the middle."

"I'm sorry Belle, I set some of this in motion. I'm partly responsible. I've got to do what I can. If we can save him, I'll take him right to the FBI. I promise."

This was entirely true as far as it went. What I didn't say was that I would do anything short of torture to find out what he knew about the ringleaders. I put my .32 in a belt holster and grabbed a cab to West 61st Street to Jimmy's rented room. Bill was loitering on the street, two buildings away. I strolled over to him and asked for a smoke while we both scanned the street around us and tried to look casual.

"Looks clear," I whispered as he lit the stale cigarette he borrowed from Chris for just this sort of pantomime, "I'll go in first. Chris still there?"

"Yup."

The boarding house was right out of a Leonard Cohen song. I'd kill myself before I'd set up housekeeping in this hovel. I found room 213 on the second floor. The door was so flimsy and ill-fitted that I was sure Chris could hear me. So I didn't bother to knock.

"Chris, it's Declan," I said in an even voice.

He opened right away. I scanned the dump quickly and moved him across the room to a closet. We stood partly inside the closet and spoke with an eye towards the door.

"We'll have to be very quiet," I whispered. "Every sound in here is clearly heard in the hall."

"I know, I've been in this closet for two hours," he continued with his maniacal grin, "I found a Louisville

Slugger in here." He held it up like a retriever looking for approval.

"Good, I'm going to settle into the bathroom with the door slightly ajar," I let him see my Walther for morale, "Bill will be up soon."

And so he was. Bill sat on a creaky pressed-back chair without attempting to hide. His back was to the window and he faced the door. Chris remained tucked away in the closet, and I manned the bathroom with my .32 at the ready. In spite of our nerves, we managed to stay deathly quiet for almost two hours. Then it paid off. We heard his footsteps a long way off. They stopped at 213. The flimsy lock opened and James was two steps into the room before he noticed Bill. He almost turned to run but Chris came out behind him and blocked his escape.

"Whaddaya want?"

"Listen James, we're here to save your miserable life. The FBI knows all about your insurance scam. Two other adjusters who were working for the same crew have been murdered. The last one was shot less than twenty four hours ago. The crooks are cleaning up their trail. You're next, buddy."

"I, I don't know what..."

Bill stood up and gave him a tremendous backhand.

"OK, asshole, we're leaving. I'm not gonna to stay here and get shot with you."

"Wait, wait, sure, I know what you're talking about. What do you want, money? Honest, I got nothing. I blew it all."

"Yeah, we know all about it. Harry the Hat says thanks. Look, we have to get out of here. I'm a newspaper man. I don't want anything but your story. Let's go..."

Timing is everything in life. Take Mohammad Ali, for example. He was incredibly fast. There were so many fights where he stood flat footed, bouncing against the ropes. He'd

The Fall of Declan Curtis

bob his head or just lean back a few strategic inches while some of the biggest hitters in the world threw blockbusters at his face. A miscalculated inch, a slight variation in his reflexive motion, and he would have been destroyed. Timing. If we had only left a few minutes sooner.

The crappy door to that hell hole splintered apart. Two fat, nasty thugs jostled each other as they tried to get through the jamb at the same time. The first one had his ridiculously large cannon unholstered. He'd seen too many Clint Eastwood movies. No one needs a gun that big unless you're hunting elephants. I stepped out of the bathroom and shot him. No time for warnings. Alas, I didn't shoot him very well; although it did keep him from shooting anyone else. Evidently, my shot ripped across the surface of his belly from left to right and went into the forearm on his shooting side. I really did intend to shoot him in center mass; but I guess I was distracted by the second thug who was aiming at me. As it turned out, I didn't have to shoot that one. Chris hit him on the back of his skull with the athletic equipment. His swing would have been good for a stand-up double. Thug Number Two wasn't completely unconscious but he dropped his gun and rested peaceably on his hands and knees for a while. He seemed to be searching intently for an answer in the floor boards. None was forthcoming.

"Billy, get a good grip on James," I didn't want him to bolt.

"Chris, gather up the cannons."

Thug Number One was staring daggers my way. It seems that no matter how fair the fight had been, crooks always hated me after I shot them. There was never any sense of sportsmanship or congratulating a fella on a job well done.

"OK, guys, what am I going to do with you?"

Neither of them seemed to have any suggestion.

"All right, get them face down on the floor, hands raised above their heads."

Our assailants didn't like this at all. How many men had they executed just this way? I walked up to my victim and pointed my Walther at his forehead.

"Don't make me kill you, asshole. Just lie down."

After they were prone and stretched, I had Chris remove their wallets and take their driver's licenses. Today's hitmen didn't seem to follow the traditional protocols of their trade.

Just like Bogo and the monsters who tortured me at the loft, they had shown up with IDs. No pride in their work. Maybe that's why they were unsuccessful? Anyway, I noticed our shooting victim's forearm wound was through and through. I'd look for the slug later.

"I suggest you two leave town. I'm going to give your licenses to the cops."

"Yeah, yeah, we're gone," said Thug Number Two. Maybe it was even true. Their boss wouldn't like hearing they blew the hit.

"What about you, asshole?" I inquired of Thug Number One. I encouraged him with a little toe to the midriff.

"Da, da, whatever," he grumbled through his pain.

I had a bad reaction, the old dead man passing through your body kind. Billy heard it, too. He passed the license to me. Alexei Agron. Shit. "Am I messing with the Russians again?" I wondered.

"Who are you thugs working for?" I attempted to yell in my best authoritative voice.

Of course, I knew it was bootless to do so, but as long as we were all there, I gave it a go.

"*Kheel* me now," my shooting victim spat out in his heavy Russian accent. As attractive as the suggestion was, I moved on.

"OK, the three of us are well armed now. Here's what I

The Fall of Declan Curtis

want you two to do. Just get up and leave the building, fast. If I don't see your lucky faces on the street from this window in about half a minute, all three of us will come down and shoot you where we find you. Come on, up! Get out, now."

They didn't know what to make of this. They tentatively backed to the smashed door. Maybe they also remembered shooting people in the back. Then they hauled themselves down the stairs like they were on fire. They didn't even look up at us as they spilled down the front steps and ran towards Ninth Avenue.

"I fired from here, so let's look around over there for my slug."

"Why does it matter? You didn't kill anyone." Bill asked.

"I'm not licensed to carry this. If I can't find the slug, I'll have to ditch my Walther. And I don't want to give it up."

"It's OK, I got it," said Chris, "it hardly had enough energy left to go into the wall."

"Excellent. Let's get up to the roof, gentlemen."

The roof of the four story tenement was a patchwork of tar flaps, plumbing vents, and small brick chimneys which had also been tarred. There was a two foot knee wall at the street side and no barrier at the back. The two sides abutted taller buildings. I told them we were up here to make sure there were no re-enforcements waiting for us on the street. That wasn't the real reason.

"Time to tell me all about it, James."

"What, what do you want to know? Seems like you know all about it already."

I told him I wanted to review all the jobs. Bill took notes and Chris took pictures. I asked a lot of questions, not in any logical sequence. I didn't want him to see where I was going with it. It took about twenty-five minutes. It turned out that Sal was his contact as well.

"Tell me about your conversations with Sal. Where did you meet, did he ever have anyone with him?"

This went on for some time without producing anything new I could use. I gave up trying to be subtle.

"All right, James, think hard. Ever hear anything about who Sal worked for?"

"No, I just gave him copies of policies with the inventories of insured valuables. They took it from there. Sometimes they would arrange to sell everything back to us, and other times we never heard from them again."

"How did you get paid?"

"They gave me a percentage of the buy-back, or a flat fee if they kept it."

"Yes, but how did you get the money?"

"In cash. They would show up without warning and give me an envelope. I never knew when."

"Think hard, James. I'd just as soon toss you off this fucking roof if I think you're holding back on me."

I dragged him to the back edge of the roof, overlooking the trash-strewn back lot. Even I was experiencing some vertigo now.

"Think, you bastard, anything Sal ever said or did to indicate who he worked for?"

He was trembling. It was clear he wasn't holding out. I pulled him back from the precipice.

"Once... once, Sal made a call from a coffee shop," James said as he scrunched his face up in an effort to recall, "I delivered a policy there. He seemed to have trouble communicating with whoever he was speaking to. He kept talking slower and louder. I overheard him mention a restaurant in Brighton Beach, Elena's. He said he would be there in an hour. That's the only time I ever heard anything. I never had more than a few words with Sal, I swear."

So, there it was, another Russian connection. Goddammit. We put James in a taxi with instructions to see Red, who would get him settled with the FBI. I told the insurance adjuster I would pay for a lawyer and have him

The Fall of Declan Curtis

meet James at Red's office.

"Just shut up about details until the lawyer gets there."

I asked James to leave out the part about the shooting and our presence in his room at all that day.

"You can tell them you were interviewed by the *Times*. Say it was at a saloon and that you know the crooks are going to kill you. After that, speak only though the shyster. Just tell them that you want to make the best deal you can and help them with their case. And tell them you want to stay alive, too."

Chapter Thirty-One
Grievous Angels

WE CLEANED UP the blood in James Coffee's room as well as we could with his sheets and took them with us. The floor wouldn't pass a luminol test if forensics ever investigated, but it would keep the landlord from reporting a bloody scene to the cops if he ever repaired the door.

"Maybe you should have gone with him to the cops, make sure he got there?" Bill said.

"He's a grown man. If he won't save himself, it's not my problem."

"I know, Deck, but the other guy wound up dead."

I think Bill felt a bit guilty for pumping Hawling for his story and then leaving him alone.

"Look, these creeps were in bed with the bad guys. We gave them a chance to get right. If they don't take it, it's not on us."

Bill looked quizzically at me. Maybe it was my conscience, but I thought I saw that "I don't know who you are" look in his eyes.

"Listen, I'm not a social worker, and neither are you. You got your big scoop and I got some info that will help me find the men who tried to kill Athena. Our mission was to find information. And if, in the course of that, we gave two mooks a chance to save themselves so be it. If we're not heroes, we are at least on the side of the angels."

"And grievous angels they are," said Bill.

I'd had quite enough excitement for one day. I headed back to Athena's apartment and gathered my things. I left a note for her to get packed and meet me at the Plaza. I told her not to tell anyone where we were staying. We'd check into our suite a few days early for our meeting with Uncle.

The Fall of Declan Curtis

That would give me a chance to unwind and also to avoid an angry interview with Red. Our interference with their investigation would not be taken calmly. I knew I'd have to see him soon enough, but I was happy to give myself a few days to prepare.

Our suite was on the fifth floor, facing the park. I told the desk to steer Athena up when she arrived. The living room windows overlooked a pair of Henry Moore bronze sculptures at the edge of the park. Athena expressed enthusiasm for them but I was unmoved. I liked the Alice in Wonderland vignette near the boathouse just fine. The park stretched out before me, a treasure befitting the island's status among the great cities of the Western world, even as every possible inch of land around it is exploited. Robert Moses, who destroyed so much of New York, suggested paving parts of Central Park to solve the parking situation in the 1950s. The barbarians are always at the gate.

A dining room opened just off the vestibule. It was an interior room with no windows, furnished with an oval table that could seat eight comfortably. The bedroom featured a king size bed with altogether too many drapes, bolsters, and pillows. There was no room for people without dumping them on the floor, which is exactly what I did after showering. Then I climbed in and passed out.

A few mumbled pleasantries and the dropping of a suitcase outside the bed room woke me around six that evening.

"Hey, sleepy, what have you been up to, and why are we hiding?"

"Well, for one thing, Bill and Chris and I just saved that last fool adjuster from being murdered. We sent him off in a cab to Red. He is probably clasped to the bosom of his lawyer and the FBI by now, and no longer my problem."

"That's wonderful, Deck, but somehow I don't feel that's the end of the story."

"Well, it probably isn't. But let's have a quiet night without thinking about it for a while. You know they have a perfectly lovely oyster bar in the basement?"

"Can we just have them sent up? I'm exhausted, myself."

"You bet. Want to shower while I put in our order?"

She answered by raising her eyebrows and prancing off to the bath on the balls of her feet. I laughed to myself. I found these occasional girlish flourishes quite charming. I put on the big hotel robe and called in an order for eighteen Malpeques and a vintage Veuve Cliquot Rose. We could decide later if dinner should be sent up, too.

After the oysters were gone and we were working on the second half of the champagne, we settled into a comfortable silence. Athena was the first to break it.

"What do you think Uncle wants?"

I was relieved that she wasn't broaching the subject I had put on hold for the evening.

"I don't know exactly. It's pretty clear that his sources are drying up in Russia. It's been a very productive five years. I still have a lot of his merchandise to sell, but the end of our business relationship is in sight."

"How will that affect you?"

"Well, it'll change the business model, but that's not a big problem. I've made enough money from our relationship to support a prudently comfortable life style indefinitely. I have some ideas for new directions, as well. With some effort on my part, everything will be quite easy from here."

"That sounds terrific, Deck. I'd love to see you living without the drama we've endured this past year."

"So, Belle, why don't you become my lawyer full time? We can travel and have an interesting life together."

"I've been thinking about that. I'll let you know when I land upon an answer."

That's what I loved about her, no fussy evasions. She states the facts simply. That's a result of thinking clearly and having confidence. These are qualities that are not common in women, or men for that matter.

"OK, I'll be here when you decide. Our dinner is in two days. I'll suggest to him that we have it downstairs in the Oak Room. I'll call this evening and confirm that it's OK with him. Meanwhile, that leaves us free tomorrow night. Do you have any interest in having dinner with Bill and Chris tomorrow if they're available?'

She agreed and we capped off the night with a carriage ride through the park.

~ ~ ~

Uncle's secretary returned my call in the morning. They would be checking in today. She confirmed the dinner at the Oak Room the next evening but asked if we could have a meeting in the morning. She said he did not like to discuss business over dinner. I knew that. I told her I had a suitable meeting room in my suite. We made our conference plans for the next morning at eleven.

~ ~ ~

That evening we met Bill and Chris at Jim Downey's Steak House.

"My Dad took me out on special occasions, birthdays and such," I told my guests, "He'd always ask what kind of food I wanted. The answer, as he well knew, was steak. By the time I was a teenager I knew every great steakhouse in Manhattan. We were leaving here one night after celebrating my thirteenth birthday. I was half way up the stairs to the street level as a cab pulled to the curb. Elizabeth Taylor stepped out. She wore a classic 60s white A-line dress with a high cinched waist and necklace that looked like it should come with a porter. But it's her sparkling eyes I remember. I froze on the step with my hand on the rail. She held my eyes and smiled at me as she descended like a queen."

"Must have been a shock for a thirteen-year-old boy," Athena said.

"Well, put it this way, my teenage girlfriends didn't have a chance after that. You're the first woman who's turned my head since then."

"Holy crap, Deck, who writes your material?" asked Bill, a bit loudly. Perhaps it was the Martinis.

"Now, Bill," Athena said, "a girl likes to be lied to a little, now and then, at least about her beauty," she smiled at me as she set up her punch line, "But he certainly is shameless, isn't he?"

The evening proceeded with similar pleasant banter. We told her about the time I blew up a bathroom with fireworks on a freshman prep school trip to D.C. We even got into our psychedelic adventures in college.

"I had a luxurious three bedroom apartment in Jersey City in 1969. On the night of a Doors concert we threw a "going away" party. Of course, we were only "going away" across the Hudson to be with Jimbo for a few hours. My roommate, Joey, had scored five tickets to the Felt Forum."

We toasted Joey.

"So," I continued, "friends came to party us off. The air shimmered with cheap Mexican pot smoke, incense, and John Cippolina's guitar. Young girls floated by in flowing colors. We had no furniture, just mattresses with Indian-print spreads. We left the blotter acid for the last half hour before takeoff. It was the hash that drove the train off the tracks. A crew of girls showed up with a ball of hash the size of a small apple; I took a big bite. I flirted with the shiny gamine who brought it. I joked about Eve and the Tree of Knowledge. Things got fuzzy in short order.

'Time to go,' I announced, 'we need to get the car parked before we start to hallucinate'.

But by the time we got to the street, I knew I couldn't

The Fall of Declan Curtis

drive. I wound up in the back seat as we headed for the Lincoln Tunnel. The car was fogged with pot. Everyone laughed as if we were on a carnival ride. I didn't. It was only I who could see that we were headed into a black maw. All the windows were down to clear the pot smell before we stopped at the tolls. We came to a halt behind a line of cars. I was ripping now, and the flashing lights over the booths freaked me out. I realized that we were surrounded and we had to give ourselves up.

'Show them your hands, man. Give it up,' I cried.

Several voices tried to calm me down.

'Don't shoot,' I said as I tried to get out of the car.

They sat on me as we paid our toll and went through.

'Wow, how did we get out of that?' I said."

Everyone was laughing at this point. Part of it was the booze, but we were truly having a jolly evening. I looked at Athena to make sure she wasn't bored.

"I was in psychic connection with everyone in the crowd at the Garden. I could hear their conversations and their innermost thoughts. Then I realized I didn't have my ticket.

'Hey, you can't leave me here alone,' I said.

Everyone else had their tickets. I was trembling. Various drugs were kicking in. I was in full panic mode. I started to pass out. Bill was bargaining with a scalper to get me a ticket. I was vaguely aware of being carried by my arms and legs through the crowd and into the arena. They dumped my unconscious carcass into a seat. We were in the eighth row, center.

'Yeeaaaahhh!' came the endless leonine bellow. Jim Morrison's scream tore through my blackout. My eyes bugged open. He was bent slightly and leaning towards the audience. He was staring right at me, his eyes locked on mine. I guess he didn't want me to miss anything."

"Well, that's a long strange trip from Liz's eyes to Jimbo's," said Chris.

"It was just six years," I said.

"Seems like you've spent a lot of your life pushing your luck, Deck," said Athena.

"I've been told that before. I guess it's true, although I never see it that way at the time."

"How did you guys ever avoid being arrested?"

"Well, Athena, not all of us did. My apartment was raided once. Bill was there, but I was in San Francisco at the time."

"Athena, he was a lucky bastard, even then," Bill said,

"Remember what Joey said to the cops?" I asked Bill.

"Yes I do, immortal lines. The cops were banging on the door. The head detective screamed, 'Nagel, Narcotics!', and without skipping a beat Joey said, 'No thanks, we already have some'. The door came down on top of him and the squad ran across it as if Joey were a troll under a bridge."

That bit of slapstick got a good laugh.

"Remember what his mother had to say?"

"Oh yeah," said Bill, "after the raid she told her son, 'Curtis is the kind of guy who always gets away with things, and you're the kind of guy who always gets caught.'"

"Ouch, Mom, thanks for the vote of confidence!" Chris said. He told a few funny stories about several of his marriages. Then we made Athena tell stories about herself. Hers involved romance and wanderlust rather than the foolishness we recounted. She had lived in Russia, Greece, and Poland. She spoke several languages. She had been a serious and successful student all her life. That may have had something to do with her professional success. We parted with many toasts.

"I really like your friends, Deck. You're all bad boys and you drink too much, but the stories are fun."

"Belle, if you can sit through a bullshit session with my old college buddies, you must love me."

Chapter Thirty-Two
The Offer

BILL CALLED at nine a.m.

"These early calls are getting to be a habit, Bill."

"Well, I waited until nine."

"That you did, my dear fellow, and god bless you for it. What's up?"

"I couldn't find an appropriate moment to fit it in last night, and a lovely time it was, but I want you to know that the first story is in today's paper."

"Indeed, how did you approach it?"

"I started with a re-cap of Bob Dexter's murder and revealed that it was connected to the big heist recovery. Then I laid out our interview with Fred Hawling and described his subsequent murder. I left out the attack on you and Athena. And I'm saving Sal's murder for the next article. Finally, I quoted James Coffee's confession detailing his part in the scheme. The exposé explains the structure of the racket. I pontificated a bit about how seemingly 'victimless' crimes turn brutal when the perpetrators are cornered. I left the reader hanging with a suggestion that we are continuing our investigation and will reveal the identity of the syndicate behind everything. It's quite a swashbuckling story, both complex and lurid. It will make a splash. Although, I suspect the insurance companies won't be thrilled."

"Bill, has it occurred to you that the 'syndicate' won't be too happy either? If you're not careful, it's you who will make a 'big splash'."

"That's rich, coming from you, Deck. When have you ever been cautious? Besides, they don't kill newsmen in this country."

The Fall of Declan Curtis

"They do in Russia," I thought to myself. I hung up, uneasy about the conversation. Of course, I knew the story would eventually be published. I just hoped that we would have had a clearer grip on the bad guys by then. What I really would have preferred was seeing them rounded up by the FBI before any "*exposés*." Then Billy's story would be the first detailed explanation of the events. He might even get a book deal out of it.

"Who was that?"

"It was Bill. The first part of his *exposé* of the insurance racket is in today's *Times*."

"Seems a bit too soon for that. Is it wise?" Athena asked.

"No."

~ ~ ~

We got a courtesy call from one of Uncle's young men, confirming that they would be on time. This was no surprise to me. I had already ordered coffee and tea and all the expected accoutrements. I included seltzer, quinine water, and limes. I tried to cover all the bases.

Everything was neatly arranged on the side board in the meeting room and the table was set. The room service men were out of our suite long before a polite knock announced Uncle's arrival. I opened the door and saw him standing between two of his young men. Another older man trailed them. Uncle smiled angelically as one of the men passed me and wandered quickly through the suite. Only then did Uncle step in and clasp my hands in his.

"A great pleasure to be with you again, my boy."

"Likewise, Uncle. I'd like to introduce you to my attorney, Athena."

"Finally, my dear, we meet. You are even more beautiful than Deck led me to believe."

"Thank you," Athena said, assuming that this flourish was the last of the Blarney.

"More importantly, he tells me you are smarter than

him. That is a wonderful thing."

"May I introduce you to my accountant, Ben Ward?" Uncle said before Athena had to find an answer to his enigmatic comment.

"Please, let's all go into the meeting room and get comfortable," I said.

Ben came in and sat down with us. There was no other door to the room, so the young men were satisfied to wait unobtrusively in the living room. I offered them coffee but they declined.

Uncle smiled a little when I offered him his usual drink of quinine and lime.

"Very thoughtful of you. Now, let us get to the purpose of this meeting. As you have observed, the supply of rugs from Russia has dwindled. It may take you another year to liquidate the last of my consignment pieces with you. But the end of our enterprise is in sight. This has been a successful venture for you and for my family. After five years, I feel like I know you as well as a business man may know another."

"I'm flattered, and I'm very appreciative of the opportunity you gave me," I said.

"Each of us has given fair value. Now, if you want to move on with your own enterprise, I know you will be successful. You have formed a capital base that will allow you to make a mark on the business as you see fit. Your real estate investment was very sound. Your catalogues and exhibitions have earned you an international profile. Bravo."

"You are too kind with your estimation. Are we here to part ways?"

"That will be entirely up to you," Uncle said as he turned towards Athena, "and your attorney. You have commented to me many times that the business of antique carpets is a very small world. You've said that a few tens of millions in capital, in the hands of a sufficiently knowledgeable man, could dominate the world market."

"Yes, I think that is the case. There are only a hundred real players in the world. Even that is a generous estimate. The mid-range material that we've been getting out of Russia is of no consequence at the top level of the business. There are great carpets that sell for hundreds of thousands , even millions, of dollars. There are very few dealers with that sort of capital. But there are many uber-wealthy people who will buy them. There is room for a well-financed expert to corner or at least seize a substantial share of that market."

"We are willing to test your hypothesis. We know you have approximately a million dollars in cash and instruments. You also have a similar value in the rugs that you own. And then there is your grand hotel. Of course, your money is your own. But we would like to buy everything else, including your exclusive services for ten years."

"I'm rather awed, Uncle," I said as I glanced at Athena. She didn't give anything away about her reaction to the deal. She just steadily jotted notes on her legal pad.

"I'm sure you are, Deck. Here's what we had in mind. We'll pay you five million dollars in cash for your inventory and hotel. You will be a multi-millionaire. Of course, you may continue to occupy your quarters in the hotel as part of your compensation."

"And how will we justify this investment?"

"We will put up a ten million dollar line of credit for you. I want you to open galleries in prime locations here and in Europe. I'd like one in Israel, too. I want it done carefully, one gallery at a time. As an operatic tenor used to say, 'Don't take a step longer than your leg'. You will have complete control of the business model and the staffing. Make it work, Deck, and you will become a rich man."

"Well, that still leaves a lot of details to work out."

"You and I have never split hairs about details. You will

have a generous expense account. All your living expenses will be covered. You may draw two hundred thousand a year plus a percentage of the sales. I suggest you hire a full time attorney, preferably one who already knows about you."

He beamed at Athena as he said this.

"OK, I think that covers the basic ideas. Your attorney can get together with Ben and work out contracts, key employee insurance, and so forth."

"Uncle, you are assuming I'll say yes."

He exploded with laughter. His eyes began to water and he drew a handkerchief and dabbed them.

"Really, Declan, you should have been a standup comedian."

That made Athena laugh. I think she liked him.

"Well, I look forward to our dinner tonight. Until then."

Ben Ward gave Athena a small stack of paper and they had a few whispered words and a handshake. Uncle gripped my hand.

"Now, the real adventure begins, my boy."

After they left Athena looked at me, wide-eyed.

"You lead a charmed life, lover. In my world, a deal like that would involve half dozen lawyers, investigations, audits and who knows what else. And, it would take many months."

"Can you handle this?"

"I'll have to read through these contracts. But I don't see why not."

"Well, I won't own anything for a while, but that's liberating in itself. And I'll be pretty rich by my standards. Why don't you become my full-time attorney? I'll see that you get an attractive salary."

"You know how I feel about you, Deck. I'm just getting comfortable with the commitment. Leaving the insurance job I don't care about is easy. Taking a job with complex emotional ties would be much harder to ever leave. It means

surrendering some autonomy."
 "You can always go. Remember, 'No hard feelings'."
 "Don't bullshit me, Mr. Curtis."

Chapter Thirty-Three
Mom

BILL LEFT the Times building after seven p.m. He was pumped up with his current project. The response to part one of his exposé of a major insurance scam was tremendous. Calls had come in for interviews from various TV stations, both news and gossip. Other papers were picking up the story from the Times. He was more than a little pleased with himself. He had a rendezvous at a Hell's Kitchen saloon with Chris, his photographer, and a bottle of Hendrick's gin.

Press noise spilled out of the block-long building as he negotiated his way around the delivery trucks backed up to the loading docks. Strong union men handled bound bundles of the day's paper early in the morning but the docks were nearly empty now. Bill had lived in the city most of his adult life and had good city instincts. This time those reflexes did him no good. The first shot came out of still darkness. He was mortally wounded even before he saw them emerge from the murk. He saw the muzzle flashes, but that was all.

"Mom," was the last thing he mumbled.

The gunmen moved quickly towards Eighth Avenue, but not quickly enough. A call had been made to the cops from the dock. Even before that could be responded to, a random patrol car took notice of the men. As it slowed near them, they panicked and ran. The cops called in and put the siren on. The biggest mistake the thugs made was firing a shot at the patrol car.

"Shots fired Eighth Avenue and 43rd street," went out over the radio.

Other cars were arriving now. Several officers were in

The Fall of Declan Curtis

pursuit on foot. They didn't want a big shoot out near the theater crowd, but when they got close they let loose. You can't expect a polite arrest when you fire at police. Both thugs went down quickly. One of them lived on the way to the hospital but was declared dead there. On the ride he talked in his delirium. He spoke in Russian to someone named Yissakhar.

Chapter Thirty-Four
"Chinatown"

"YES," SHE SAID, "yes."

I felt pressure on my chest. I opened my eyes.

"Yes!"

I began to focus. Her elfin face, the one she saved for private moments, looked down at me through her long raven hair. She had straddled me and leaned her palms on my chest.

"Yes is good, yes back at you. Now, what the hell did we just agree to?"

"I'm quitting the insurance company. You have a full time attorney. And even if this deal with Uncle doesn't go through, I'm still casting my lot with you, Declan Curtis."

That brought the world into sharp focus. I wrestled her off me and we had our ways with each other for a blissful hour. Then I ordered an absurdly large breakfast while she showered. By the time I stepped out of my shower, she was in the midst of a smoked salmon omelet.

"You've got jam on your lip," I kissed it off, "mmm, apricot, my favorite."

"The world looks different today," she said as she sipped her mimosa.

"Yes, things seem to be taking shape nicely," I said as I joined her in our first breakfast as an official team.

"Why do you suppose Uncle has such serious security? He seems like a head of state or a Mafia don."

"I really don't know," I said, "but of course you're right. I suppose he is a bit of both of those things. He's the head of a big family of international traders, manufacturers, and investors. He's never hinted at any illegal activities, but even legitimate business can get rough at times. I have no

The Fall of Declan Curtis

idea who his enemies might be."

"It's so mysterious. Have you ever asked him?"

"No, no I haven't. You've been with him in person now. Don't you sense he's not a person to press?"

"I understand what you're saying. But if you're, I mean 'we're', going to be in bed with him, perhaps you should be more inquisitive?"

"You are quite right in theory. However, I'll bet he would gladly give us an exhaustive file about himself and his enterprises. In fact, I will ask him to do just that. But I guarantee, no amount of independent research will turn up anything more than he wants us to have. That's just how careful he is. I decided a long time ago to follow my instinct and trust him. It has been very much to my benefit. And I've had no cause to suspect anything underhanded."

An aggressive rap on our door disturbed our conversation. Normally, we were called from the desk if someone wanted to visit. I thought it was probably one of Uncle's young men. I was mistaken.

"Red, come on in."

He was red both in name and complexion this morning.

"What the hell do you think you're doing? If you were anyone else, I'd arrest you for obstructing our investigation."

"Well, it's a good thing I have my attorney here," I said, trying to introduce a bit of levity. It was a mistake.

"Not the time, boyo," he warned me.

"I'm sorry, Red. Look, the *Times* reporter was doing an investigation of the robberies. I knew him from school. When he read about the attack on me he got in touch. Yes, I helped him connect the dots. But in the end you got James Coffee and his confession. That must be worth something."

Yes, I know, I was still prevaricating. Bill didn't come to me, I went to him. But I was trying to make the story more palatable to Red.

"What we do isn't a game. Eventually, we would've gotten the whole story. And Fred Hawling might still be alive."

"I'm truly sorry, Red."

"Well, I'm sorry too, Declan. I'm sorry because I know you are a good man and this will be hard to live with. Your friend Bill is dead, too."

I'd like to say I'd take that sort of news like Humphrey Bogart. I'd stuff my thumbs in my vest pockets, twitch my lips a few times, and ask, "How'd he get it?" The truth is, I went to the bathroom and blew all that lovely breakfast. Jesus Christ, is this all my fault? I looked at my face in the mirror. I looked deranged. If I hadn't gone to him with the story, Bill would have been drinking with Chris tonight and arguing about the Rolling Stones. Sure, it was his job. And sure, he ran the story too soon. But once again I was at the vortex of a tragedy.

"Sorry," I said as I re-entered the room. Athena had tears on her face as she held me by the waist. I thought they were mostly for me, and the burden she knew I would carry over this.

"Red, may I ask you how it went down?"

"Two shooters got him at the *Times* Building loading docks around six p.m."P He never knew what hit him. Both of them were killed by police. They were Russians. We know exactly who they were, part of the same mob that tried to kill you five years ago. The boss who was after you then was killed by one of his own men. These two worked for the big boss, Yissakhar, they call him 'The Bear'."

Red had looked hard at me when he talked about Oleg being killed by his "own man". Red knew very well that Bogo wasn't alive to do that hit. That was our little secret. But I wondered if he suspected the truth? The only fire wall I had between myself and that suspicion was the sheer outlandishness of the idea of me as a hit man.

The Fall of Declan Curtis

"Now, I'm only going to say this once, Deck. And this goes for you, too, counselor. If either of you interfere in any way in this case again, I swear I will throw you in jail. And while you're pondering that, mull this over, you may be back on their radar now. I strongly suggest you both take a long vacation until this blows over."

"Will you need us to give statements?"

"I don't think so, Deck. The NYPD is reduced to picking off peripheral players, caught in the act. We've never gotten at the Russian mobs. Remember the movie 'Chinatown'? There's no way in. Maybe after another generation there will be 'Americanized' members who can be turned. But their current soldiers are recruited from Russian prisons. They're the hardest core."

"So, what does that mean for Bill?"

"It means his killers are dead. That's something."

"That's like arresting the car in a hit and run and letting the driver escape."

"Maybe the Feds will get the bosses eventually."

"Red, it's not right," I said.

"That's the way it is. It's 'Chinatown'. I could lie to you and say we're on the Bear's trail but I won't bullshit you. Please get this lesson and stay out of the deep water. It's not a game, Deck. Just get out of town for a while. I don't want to bury you."

"We are getting out of town. We're opening a gallery in Europe. We'll be there for a few months finding a location."

"Congratulations, I'm truly happy for you. Enjoy your lives."

~ ~ ~

An oppressive silence descended on the room as I closed the door behind Red. I resisted the urge to break something. I needed to assure Athena that things were under control.

"Deck?"

"It's all right. We'll get through this. I really can't talk about this now. Let's get ready for our meeting with Uncle."

Athena had read through the papers. They didn't cover all the details but they were specific and generous. Uncle wanted both of us to hire accounting firms to watch the books. That way, he said, "we'll have an eye on the accountants, as well as each other." I would have no ownership or presence in the corporation. I was strictly an employee. Aside from my base salary, expense account, and other perks my percentage was not specified. No matter what form that took, I was looking at a luxurious life for the next ten years. And if I invested a few of the five million I was to be paid up front, there would be a tidy sum when I "retired" in ten years.

"Welcome, I hope you are both well," Uncle said with convincing sincerity, "let's just sit here in my living room. No need for a conference table today. I assume you have read the proposal?"

"I have", said Athena, "there are only a few questions I have."

"I'm sure there are more than a few," Uncle said with a smile.

"Well," Athena began before Uncle held up his hand.

"I suggest that Deck's percentage be five per cent of the gross, annually. The enterprise should be grossing at least five million after the first new gallery is running. I'm expecting things to grow exponentially as new locations open and our influence on the world market matures. We're going to incorporate in Switzerland. If you two will join us there, everything will be finalized. Have I left anything important out, Athena?"

"No, the rest is minor. I'm sure Ben Ward and I will work it out easily."

"Deck, for a man whose fortune has just been made, you seem rather underwhelmed," Uncle said.

"I'm very grateful for this opportunity, Uncle. If I seem morose, it is because a close friend was murdered last night."

"Yes, the reporter from the *Times*. Very sad."

"Is there anything you don't already know?"

"Very little, my boy, and those few items are not important. I understand from some of my sources that it was the Russian mob that was behind the scheme your friend was writing about."

"You are well informed. The police told me it was a mob that you and I knew about once upon a time," I said obliquely, so as not to give anything words that should stay silent.

Uncle leaned forward and propped his forearms on his knees.

"Do you want me to help?"

I deeply trusted this man and had a strong urge to ask for help. I thought of the 70s song, "Send lawyers, guns and money, Dad." I was sure he would do anything to help me. But I knew just enough about the world now to know I would lose something to him. If I let him become part of what I had to do, he would always have that on me. I thought again about Ben Franklin's formula for keeping a secret.

"No, Uncle, I'll just have to live with it, no matter what I decide."

"You know best what you must do. I sincerely hope we see you in Zurich."

That wish had layers of meaning. I hoped Athena missed it. I knew he was telling me that he hoped I survived.

We checked out of the Plaza in the morning. Athena gave immediate notice at the insurance company and packed her things from the apartment. We flew to Boston and Gus picked us up. Over the next few days I managed to convince her to go to Europe with my power of attorney and

John Jeremiah

conclude the agreements with Uncle. Then I wanted her to visit a few cities and scout locations for the gallery, analyzing as well the tax implications in each country. She had a company credit card and drew a substantial cash advance for expenses. I convinced her that after concluding certain business dealings before I left, I would meet her in Vienna in three weeks.

After putting her on a plane to Zurich, I arranged with my private lawyer to transfer my wealth to Athena in the event of my death.

Chapter Thirty-Five
Bonhoeffer's Leap

EACH DAY I commuted by subway from Athena's *pied a terre* to Sheepshead Bay. I had two weeks to decide what I had to do and how to do it. Obviously, it would have been more convenient to get a hotel room there, but I didn't want to leave any trail. If Yissakhar disappeared now, even Red might start looking into my whereabouts. This had to be spotless.

That is not to say I had decided upon a plan of action. My fate seemed inextricably tied up with this gang. I thought of the Earp brothers and their problems a hundred years ago. They were plagued by a gang called "The Cowboys." Although the brothers had local law enforcement credentials, the gang managed to kill one Earp brother and maim another. The gang made several attempts on Wyatt's life. Local law enforcement didn't back him up. So, Wyatt got a Federal posse together and went after the gang, ruthlessly killing at least four of them. Murder warrants were then issued against Wyatt by corrupt local officials, and he had to leave for California. Most of the perpetrators went unpunished. Both times he was officially on the side of the law, but was treated like a criminal. In a world of corruption and influence pedaling, "right" was a capricious concept, and so it seemed now. The Russians had tried to kill me more than once, and they might yet have another go at me and the woman I loved. But they were safe in their "Chinatown" maze. The law only seemed able to clean up afterwards. How far could I go to preserve our safety and my sense of morality?

I built a file about Yissakhar at the New York Public Library. There were various stories about investigations

The Fall of Declan Curtis

and assorted allegations. He was even brought to trial once on extortion, but several witnesses recanted and one disappeared. His web of crime stretched to Eastern Europe, into Russia, and into a complex web of prison gangs and internecine rivalries. The most useful data I found were a series of photos of Yissakhar at his trial. I could identify my man.

~ ~ ~

In the mornings I walked the boardwalk and ate ham and egg sandwiches on hard Kaiser rolls from a diner. I drank orange juice because I liked it and because their coffee was undrinkable. The late summer breeze off the Atlantic was soothing. Even the gulls sounded like a sort of music. And I re-worked my dark thoughts in the midst of this gritty but bucolic scene.

It was easy to discover which yacht club Yissakhar belonged to. There were only a few of them and they had been on the waterfront in Sheepshead Bay since the nineteenth century. Coney Island was just a sandy barrier beach until Brooklyn filled in the channel to make the island part of the mainland. The parts they did not fill in became the "bay". It was full of fishing boats and pleasure craft owned by working class people. Then the Russians came into the area.

Now there were fancy boats and Russian restaurants and shops. Yissakhar's fishing yacht was a sixty-five foot Hatteras convertible. It had a pilot house above with a small deck and a bigger deck at the water level. The name on the stern was Медведь, The Bear.

I won't deny that simply leaving for our new life and forgetting about this evil was tempting. On one level, it made perfect sense. But even if they never came after us, I would still hear Bill's laugh and see his face when I closed my eyes. Dietrich Bonhoeffer took deadly steps against the evil of his time. He conspired to murder Hitler. The Fuhrer saw to it that he died in a concentration camp. The Lutheran theologian did not have the imprimatur of authority, but said that *"...when a man takes guilt upon himself in responsibility, he imputes his guilt to himself and no one else. He answers for it...Before other men he is justified by dire necessity; before himself he is acquitted by his conscience, but before God he hopes only for grace."*

I had no illusion that my enemies were as monumental as his. But I faced evil nonetheless. It had tortured me, tried to shoot me, and set me on fire. It had murdered my dear friend and tried to kill my lover. So I would take Bonhoeffer's leap. I had the further advantage of not imagining that there was a god whose grace I required. So, I'd take my chances in men's eyes and with my own conscience.

I dressed in a tee shirt, sweat pants, a Yankee cap, and sneakers. I felt invisible in the crowd as I tried to get a sense of Yissakhar's patterns. The first time I saw him come out of his office, he had two body guards and a driver. Over the course of a week, he walked to the yacht club twice. He had one body man with him the first time and two on the second trip. I remembered Oleg's speech about how easy it is to kill anyone. Of course, that assumes you are willing to go into battle with a team. Morally, I didn't want to involve anyone in these decisions. I wouldn't drag anyone else into this dark realm. On a practical level, I didn't want anyone to have that information about me. Of course, I had discovered Oleg's solution to that quibble was to murder everyone who helped him. Obviously, that solution was unthinkable.

Yissakhar never seemed to be alone. If I were to get at him without a major fire fight, it would have to be serendipitous. I played a little game with myself. I was always armed and ready. But if the chance did not arise, I would fly off to Vienna. I didn't tell myself I'd never settle with Yissakhar if that were the case. But it was wiser to forgo

The Fall of Declan Curtis

the confrontation than force it under poor conditions and fail. I tailed his entourage to several glitzy restaurants. Those nights seemed to hold the least promise. He would come out drunk in the small hours, but always in a cocoon of armed flunkies.

That night, women changed the routine. Just before two a.m. on a Monday morning, Yissakhar came out of Elena's with two curvaceous Eastern European girls. They had clearly been sewn into their brightly colored dresses. They tottered on impossibly high heels as their lithe bodies strained against their tight habiliment. Evidently, everything he said to them was exceedingly funny. His crew escorted him to the yacht and there he sent them away. He wanted to be alone with his ladies.

I expected at least one goon to stand guard on the dock. The pier only held two boats. "The Bear" was moored closest to the boardwalk. Surveillance was simple. I sat calmly on a boardwalk bench about thirty yards from the boat. His thugs could have easily protected him. They only needed to leave one man.

But no, everyone was sloppy that night, the night I finished my business and said goodbye to Sheepshead Bay. It was around 4 a.m. when he came on deck alone to have a smoke. I stood up and slowly emptied my Walther as I walked towards him. I unconsciously synced the shots with my footsteps. He slid down onto the deck in momentary astonishment. His life slipped away. The noise faded into deafening silence. The *ersterbend* was hypnotic. No one came out to see what was happening.

I breathed the cold morning air deep into my lungs and slouched off to Bethlehem.

Chapter Thirty-Six
Cyanide or Champagne

"ALONE TONIGHT?" Emile asked as I boarded the barge that houses the River Café.

The matchboard woodwork, shiny brass fixtures and vaulted ceiling all contributed to the nautical atmosphere. A cozy bar filled a corner facing the open bay and the Statue of Liberty. The windows on the river side opened onto a bustling river scene with boats and barges and water taxis churning the East River. On the opposite shore, the South Street Seaport stood, one of the last enclaves of brick Federal Period New York. The mammoth bulk of the Brooklyn Bridge loomed overhead.

"Indeed, I am, Emile. Any chance you can let me have a window?"

They saved the windows for couples and tourists.

"I think we can do that, Mr. Curtis," Emile said, flashing a covert nod to me. "May I get you a drink?"

I thought of Cole Porter's line, "Shall I order cyanide, or order champagne?" I ordered the twenty-five-year-old Macallan, my version of a celebration. I sat with my back to the bridge.

The sun was just about down behind the statue. I didn't know what I felt at this point. I had a woman's interest. She was beautiful, accomplished, and smarter than me. My deal with Uncle had made me a multi-millionaire. My future held the promise of glamorous international business and travel. And yet, I felt as if my life were over.

"Are you ready to look at a menu?" My waiter asked for a second time.

"Oh, pardon me, I was far away. Yes, please."

I perused old favorites. I would definitely have the *foie*

gras with a finely ground mist of coffee bean on top. For the rest, I was indifferent, even passing on wine. In the end, the superb food was ashes in my mouth. It was only the whiskey I tasted. I thought of Athena enjoying her European travel while scouting gallery locations for us. We were scheduled to meet at the Hotel Sacher in Vienna next week. It was a short walk from the Opera House and we had tickets for Bellini's *I Puritani*, one of my favorites. Would I be able to slip right into my old skin and conduct the delightful multi-ring circus of art and commerce that Uncle and I were creating?

"I think that's all for me. Will you bring a check, please?"

Emile arrived before the waiter could bring the check.

"Was everything to your satisfaction Mr. Curtis?" Emile asked with just the right amount of dramatic concern. He had obviously seen my uneaten food.

"Yes, Emile, it was lovely. I'm just a bit off my feed tonight."

"Next time, chef will do something very special for you," Emile said with a wide flourish of his arms.

"Well, I'll certainly look forward to that, my friend. Good night to you."

I left the barge and walked through the secluded garden they had created around the cobblestone courtyard. In spite of the bridge traffic high overhead, the garden was peaceful, even mysterious in the shadows. Festive lines of lights were draped through the trees. The winding paths were furnished with benches. I enjoyed my stroll, emerged onto the ancient street, and began to walk up towards Cadman Park to the pedestrian entrance to the Bridge. The dramatic pattern created by steel cables rising from the deck and climbing to the Gothic towers has been photographed and painted hundreds of times. But like other great monuments, it still has the power to thrill and impress in person and even make it feel like your personal discovery.

Manhattan glittered on the other side. "Baghdad on the Hudson" they called it a hundred years ago. I passed under the first arch. It is said that these two stone towers will stand after all else is gone, like the Pyramids and the Sphinx. This vast wonderland had arisen in spite of the pervasive corruption of nineteenth-century society. Despite street gangs, Tammany Hall, and the suborning of the manifold extensions of civic authority, progress plowed on. Majestic architecture and institutions -financial, political and cultural- were all born and reborn. Creative destruction and cyclical reformation produced a net gain for civilization.

Well, all of this was fermenting in my mind and my conscience. At the mid-point of the bridge, I leaned on the parapet and fixed my gaze upon the Statue of Liberty's torch and the gauzy stars above it. Can I live with these things I have done? Was there something inside of me, something that no one else could see, that was rotting away like Dorian Gray's portrait?

For a hundred years my family never lived far from the Statue. I was the first to move away from these islands where we landed. My grandmother had childhood memories of Sunday dinners on Joralemon Street with Roebling, the engineer who built this bridge. I thought of my forebears who were laborers, cabinet makers, commercial artists and elevator operators. Had any of them killed a man? I imagined convening a jury of these peers to judge me.

"Your honor, I submit to the court that these scoundrels needed killing. They were responsible for many capital crimes, corruption and serious mayhem."

I drew the Walther PP out of my pocket and expelled the clip. With my handkerchief, I carefully wiped it before dropping it off the bridge. I had used this weapon on

The Fall of Declan Curtis

Yissakhar; it had to go away. I looked at the pistol for the last time. Two extra initials were engraved into the handle: "R.J.". They stood for *Reichs Justiz*, indicating that the gun was issued to a policeman. His duty was to protect and defend the people and the peace while wearing a swastika and rounding up victims for the camps. Official justice, indeed. Well, my uncle had relieved him of his pistol "when he didn't need it any more". Perhaps I could get a "not guilty" out of my father's brother if he were on my jury.

After wiping the Walther clean, I let it slip over the edge into the East River. I didn't need it any more either.

❈ ❈ ❈

Thank you for reading.
Please review this book. Reviews help others find Absolutely Amazing eBooks and inspire us to keep providing these marvelous tales.

If you would like to be put on our email list to receive updates on new releases, contests, and promotions, please go to AbsolutelyAmazingEbooks.com and sign up.

*Many thanks to my beta readers.
And thanks to Bill Scheller who consulted and
held my hand through this whole project.
Thanks to my line editor, Anne Rugh.*

*Small excerpts from this novel were published in
Akashic Books' "Mondays are Murder" series.*

Painting by Frank Corso

About the Author

John Jeremiah is the product of a Jesuit education which equipped him to take any side of an argument. He hitchhiked around the USA and spent time following the Grateful Dead and trying to write short stories. His wanderings brought him to an old colonial seaport town on the Massachusetts coast. He fell in with a group of artists, writers and musicians who occupied semi-abandoned mill buildings. Eventually, he made his living restoring 17th and 18th century homes. After being disastrously burned in a house fire, he turned to the more genteel trade of antique dealer. This led to a growing expertise in antique oriental rugs. He spent many years as a gallery owner and international traveler and trader in old Persian carpets. He wrote and lectured extensively on that subject and is an internationally recognized expert. Four of his short stories have recently been published on Akashic Books' website. He is an alum of the Yale Writers' Conference in 2014 and 2015, where he workshopped part of this novel. A second book about Declan Curtis is in the works.

ABSOLUTELY AMAZING eBOOKS

AbsolutelyAmazingEbooks.com

or AA-eBooks.com

CPSIA information can be obtained
at www.ICGtesting.com
Printed in the USA
LVOW10s1405030417
529435LV00010B/188/P